M000309093

HE GRI... "What's the matter? Did my .... drive your fiancé right out of your mind?"

"You shouldn't have done that," she said, tying the belt of her robe around her waist with shaking hands.

"Do what, honey? Kiss you?" His eyes glittered dangerously. "Sorry, but you'll have to get a court order to stop me from doing it again and even then you may have some trouble."

"But *why*?"

"Because," he said softly, "I can't seem to get enough of the way you respond to me."

WHAT ARE *LOVESWEPT* ROMANCES?

They are stories of true romance and touching emotion. We believe those two very important ingredients are constants in our highly sensual and very believable stories in the LOVESWEPT line. Our goal is to give you, the reader, stories of consistently high quality that may sometimes make you laugh, sometimes make you cry, but are always fresh and creative and contain many delightful surprises within their pages.

Most romance fans read
Those they

...a an enormous number of books. ...truly love, they keep. Others may be traded with friends and soon forgotten. We hope that each LOVESWEPT romance will be a treasure—a "keeper." We will always try to publish

LOVE STORIES YOU'LL NEVER FORGET BY AUTHORS YOU'LL ALWAYS REMEMBER

The Editors

The Damaron Mark:

THE
BRIDE

FAYRENE
PRESTON

BANTAM BOOKS
NEW YORK · TORONTO · LONDON · SYDNEY · AUCKLAND

THE DAMARON MARK: THE BRIDE
A Bantam Book / November 1995

LOVESWEPT *and the wave design are registered trademarks of
Bantam Books, a division of Bantam Doubleday Dell Publishing Group,
Inc. Registered in U.S. Patent and Trademark Office and elsewhere.*

All rights reserved.
Copyright © 1995 by Fayrene Preston.
Back cover art copyright © by Vittorio Dangelico.
Floral border by Joyce Kitchell.
*No part of this book may be reproduced or transmitted in any
form or by any means, electronic or mechanical,
including photocopying, recording, or by any
information storage and retrieval system, without
permission in writing from the publisher.
For information address: Bantam Books.*

*If you purchased this book without a cover you should be
aware that this book is stolen property. It was reported as
"unsold and destroyed" to the publisher and neither the
author nor the publisher has received any payment for this
"stripped book."*

*If you would be interested in receiving protective vinyl covers for your
Loveswept books, please write to this address for information:*

Loveswept
Bantam Books
P.O. Box 985
Hicksville, NY 11802

ISBN 0-553-44419-0

Published simultaneously in the United States and Canada

*Bantam Books are published by Bantam Books, a division of Bantam Dou-
bleday Dell Publishing Group, Inc. Its trademark, consisting of the words
"Bantam Books" and the portrayal of a rooster, is Registered in U.S.
Patent and Trademark Office and in other countries. Marca Registrada.
Bantam Books, 1540 Broadway, New York, New York 10036.*

PRINTED IN THE UNITED STATES OF AMERICA
OPM   0 9 8 7 6 5 4 3 2 1

PROLOGUE

She looked like a statue as she sat on the bench in the garden beneath the full silver moon. Her skin was as pale as alabaster, her hair was paler than the moonlight. In her long white gown she was utterly still, utterly beautiful.

Too beautiful to be real.

Moments before, the sight of her had brought Cale to a stop and now he couldn't force himself to move. He was mesmerized by her. Michelangelo could have carved her. She might even be a goddess come down to earth.

He had obviously stepped into a dream.

Except the stirring in his loins was very real.

Some distance behind him, music spilled out of the big house into the night. A party was in full swing there, but in the garden the melodic sounds were muted and peace coexisted with a heavy, fragrant sensuality.

He didn't move, he didn't even think he breathed, but he must have done something, because she turned her head and looked at him.

He expected her to tense, but she didn't. Nor did she appear to be alarmed or offended.

"Yes?" she asked, her voice husky and calm.

"I didn't mean to interrupt you."

"I don't own the garden."

"So that means you aren't a Caldwell?" He gestured behind him toward the house.

"No, I'm a guest of the Caldwells."

"I'm not."

"You crashed?" There was no surprise in her tone, no censure.

"No." He waited for her to ask the next obvious question. She didn't, and silence fell between them. The silence wasn't strained, but he wanted to hear her voice again, wanted to learn more about her. "Did you get tired of the party?"

"The people."

"You got tired of all of them?"

A weary smile touched her lips. "Some of them." She paused, her gaze focused somewhere far away. "There was no air in there."

"Last time I looked the party was going on in a room ninety feet long with doors every fifteen feet that open out onto the terrace."

She tilted her head, causing her long pale

hair to spill over one bare shoulder. "Are you an architect?"

"No, but I can measure distance."

"What a handy talent."

She wasn't being sarcastic. In fact he had the distinct impression a part of her mind was still focused on something else and it bothered him. Unreasonably he wanted *all* of her attention.

He sat down on the bench beside her, careful not to brush against her. "It's a beautiful night, isn't it?"

"Yes," she said in her absent, preoccupied way.

Her mind had wandered away from him, and he found the idea intolerable. The night was bewitching. The moonlight was bleaching the color from the roses, but nothing could repress their sweet fragrance nor diminish the mystery and the unintentional seductiveness of the woman beside him.

"Look at me," he said softly.

Obediently she turned her face back to him. "Yes?"

"I don't want anything from you."

Faint surprise crossed her lovely face, but then was gone. "It never occurred to me that you did."

"There was something in your voice . . ." He shook his head. "Never mind." He'd been wrong, he thought. He very much wanted something from her, something that was manifesting itself in him as an ache. He held out his hand. "I'm Cale."

"Cale," she said, shaking his hand, "I'm Jo."

He kept her hand in his, needing to extend the contact with her a little longer.

It didn't seem to bother her. In fact he had the feeling that nothing was touching her, not even him. She was as remote as the statue he had mistaken her for. He laid his other hand on top of hers, completely enveloping her hand. "When I first saw you I didn't think you were real."

Something flickered in her silvery eyes. "I'm very real."

"Are you?" He studied her for a moment, then on impulse said, "Convince me." He leaned toward her and pressed his lips against hers. Amazingly she didn't resist. It was a soft kiss, a gentle kiss. It was also an extraordinarily electric kiss that sent heat shooting straight through him. He lifted his head and stared down at her. Her serene expression had finally changed, he saw with satisfaction. She was looking at him in puzzlement. "You felt that, too, didn't you? That electricity?"

She blinked. "No."

"You're lying."

"That's an odd thing to say," she said slowly. "You don't even know me."

"I know your name is Jo, and I know how you kiss. The rest I can pick up as we go along." He believed what he was saying. This moment with this woman made perfect sense to him, and in his experience moments that made perfect sense were rare. Once again he lowered his mouth to hers, only this time with pressure. Her lips tasted like honey, her skin felt like satin and smelled sweeter than the flowers around them. He gathered her closer and deepened the kiss, and a wildfire of desire raced through him. The feel of her, the scent of her, *everything* about her, was all going to his head and infiltrating his bloodstream to the point that it was hard to think of anything else.

And slowly but surely she responded to him. Bone by bone, muscle by muscle she softened against him. Exhilaration surged through him. He'd broken through her remoteness. Finally he'd *really* touched her.

She was like a flame in his arms, shimmering brightly and hotly and growing wilder as the moments passed. He could feel the pressure of her fingers as they clutched the shoulders of his jacket, feel her breasts as they pressed against his chest. She wasn't far away anymore. She was here, with him, totally involved, wanting him. And suddenly he was burning up with need for her. "Open your mouth," he rasped. *"Please."*

She tensed, but only briefly, and then she

did as he asked, and when his tongue slipped into her mouth she moaned.

"God," he said with a hoarse breath against her open lips. "Where did you come from? How did I get so damned lucky to find you?"

She stiffened, going rigid against him.

"Jo?"

She wedged her hands between them and pushed against his chest. "I can't do this."

"Do what?" His brow creased. "You mean, kiss me?"

Panic flashed into her eyes and then just as quickly disappeared. "I've got to go."

"No, wait—" He tried to grab her hand, but she was too quick for him.

She rose and took off running toward the house, her white gown flaring out around her as she ran. Rose petals fell as she passed, leaves fluttered. And then right before his eyes she vanished into the moonlight.

ONE

Cale was still thinking about the woman named Jo the next day as he drove up the long tree-lined drive, his destination the sprawling stone mansion that loomed up ahead of him. He had an appointment with Abigail Damaron, the matriarch of the formidable and vastly powerful Damaron family, to discuss his providing security for her great-niece's wedding. Even though he had more or less inherited the Damaron account from his uncle, the job wasn't a fait accompli.

But as important as the Damaron account was to him, he couldn't keep his mind on it.

If it hadn't been for the kisses he and Jo had shared, he would have thought he had dreamed her. But the kisses had been all too real; proof was the restless night he had spent, tossing and turning, remembering and reliving their encounter.

He was going to find her again—there was no question in his mind. As soon as he was through with this appointment he was going to drive over to the Caldwells' and ask a few discreet questions. And if that didn't work, he'd damned well forget about being discreet.

Women didn't usually stay on his mind. They didn't bother or disturb him. Oh, he had the normal sexual needs, maybe above normal. And he had had quite a few relationships that had lasted several months or more, but in the end he had always been the one to say goodbye, parting friends when possible and when it wasn't, simply parting.

Consistently his main focus had been on his work. When he was in the mood he dated and if it was right, there was sex. When he wasn't in the mood, he was perfectly happy with his own company. In fact most times he preferred it. Kissing Jo in the moonlight had been an extremely uncharacteristic thing for him to do.

And now he couldn't get the kisses or her out of his mind.

He pulled his car to a stop in front of the house and got out. A tough-looking young man in his twenties with a no-nonsense expression on his face ushered him into the house.

"Mrs. Damaron is in the sunroom," he said, turning his back on Cale and walking away with a catlike grace and a formidable assurance. "Follow me."

Cale's lips quirked. Obviously, it never occurred to the young man that he wouldn't be obeyed. He knew he could physically make someone do as he wanted, even if they weren't so inclined.

But actually Cale would have followed him even if it hadn't been in his best interest, because he was curious about the stranger. His brown hair was done in a myriad of long, gleaming Rastafarian braids that were pulled back from his face and tied with one braid. With intense golden eyes and skin the color of old copper, his looks were so exotic, he could be a blend of any number of races. He wore expensive taupe slacks with an ordinary white cotton short-sleeved T-shirt and a wildly colored pair of suspenders. Interesting butler, Cale reflected.

After leading the way down a long hallway he opened a set of double doors and waved Cale in. "Mr. Whitfield to see you."

Cale had only a moment to register the large room filled with sunshine, plants, and deeply cushioned furniture before he heard an exuberant, quickly cadenced voice say, "Thank you, David. Hello, Mr. Whitfield. Cale, isn't it? May I call you Cale? Come join me for my morning coffee."

Cale's gaze zeroed in on the tall, older

woman wearing a bright red silk caftan and holding an empty bejeweled foot-long cigarette holder. She was sitting amid a pile of brightly colored flowered pillows on a white wicker settee. She was in her late sixties, he guessed, and her handsome looks had to have been enhanced by plastic surgery, just as the flaming red hair piled high on her head owed everything to dye.

If he hadn't already known that she had married into the Damaron family, the lack of the Damaron mark—a silver streak of hair in all those who were Damarons by blood— would have told him.

The family had never offered an explanation for the mark, but other people felt free to. It was said by the world at large that fate had given the silver streak to the Damarons as an outward symbol of the grief and pain they would have to endure to balance out the great power and wealth they would earn. Yet unlike other mortals their hair never grayed beyond the single streak.

"My doctor tells me I shouldn't drink so much caffeine, but since I happen to know that my blood pressure is better than his I ignore him." Her bright blue eyes twinkled with a wonderful mischievousness as she indicated the chair opposite her. "He also told me I need to stop drinking Scotch, but I ignore him on that too. I gave up smoking for heaven sakes. What does he want?"

There was the sound of a throat being cleared, and Abigail sent the young man a narrow look. "I have as *good* as given up cigarettes." She looked back at Cale. "Mostly. Bert is a good doctor and he means well, but I know my body better than he does." The twinkle became more pronounced. "Although he does keep trying to know my body better—the old fool. He thinks he's in love with me. He's been thinking it for about thirty years—isn't that right, David?"

"That's right."

Cale turned his head and saw that the young man was leaning back against the closed double doors, his muscled arms folded across his broad chest, as if he were guarding the doors, the room, and her. Okay, so maybe he was a bodyguard.

She laughed. "David says I'm one hot mama. By the way, did you meet David? Whenever he's around my life is infinitely easier and much more amusing."

Easier? Perhaps David was an assistant. More amusing? A companion? "We hadn't met, at least not officially, Mrs. Damaron." Cale nodded at the stone-faced David and earned a megawatt smile from Abigail Damaron for the effort.

"Call me Abigail, Cale. Everyone does. Coffee?"

Enjoying the show that was Mrs. Abigail Damaron, he settled back in the chair. "That would be nice. Black, please."

She poured the coffee from a heavy-looking sterling silver pot into a fragile china cup. "So you're Raymond's nephew?"

"Yes," he said, rising briefly to take the coffee cup from her. "My father is his brother." Unable to help himself he threw another glance at David. He hadn't moved or changed expressions.

"Raymond gave you his unqualified approval. He said you're the very best there is."

"I appreciate him saying that."

Her cigarette holder sliced through the air. "Believe me, he wouldn't have said it if you didn't have the credentials to back you up. Master's degree from MIT, a former secret service agent—Raymond is very proud of you."

"That's kind of him."

"Nonsense. With your background, it was very natural that he invite you to take over his business when he decided to retire. He also said that you've brought with you some of the latest technology and have improved the business to a remarkable degree."

"I like to think I have."

"Oh, I'm sure you have. Raymond wouldn't lie to me. He and I go way back." The cigarette holder made a series of circles in the air. "In fact we had a marvelous affair one spring in Paris. Did he tell you about it?"

"Uh, no."

Cale saw a flash of long nails painted the color of her hair and her caftan as she gestured with her free hand. "Raymond was always very discreet."

Apparently, Cale thought, amused.

"It was, of course, before I married my Eugene."

Eugene Damaron, one of the fabled Damaron brothers who had helped perpetuate the family's far-flung business interests and make them even more wealthy than before. If Cale remembered correctly, Eugene Damaron had died twenty years ago and Abigail was the last of that particular generation. Now the current generation of Damarons had a firm control on the family's empire.

"About my great-niece's wedding," Abigail said, then frowned to herself. "As far as I'm concerned this interview is really just a formality, but you do need to meet the bride-to-be to make sure we have her approval. David, where is she? I told her about this meeting, didn't I?"

"Sure did," he said in a soft drawl. "I'm sure she'll be here any minute."

With a nod of agreement, Abigail looked back at Cale. "Joanna is always very prompt. She's also very efficient, which is why—"

The door opened, and Cale turned to see a tall, slim young woman strolling into the room. She was wearing white linen slacks, a white silk blouse, and white leather sandals. Her long arctic-blond hair was tied back at the nape with a pale gold silk scarf, and her silvery green eyes had an absent, faraway expression.

A sick feeling moved through him, followed immediately by an unreasonable, strong anger.

This was Jo, the woman he had kissed last night in the moonlight. And apparently it was her wedding for which he would be providing security.

"Oh, good, Joanna, you're here." Abigail greeted her with a warm smile. "Darling, come meet Cale Whitfield. He's Raymond Whitfield's nephew and from what Raymond says, he's quite wonderful."

If Cale hadn't been watching Jo so intently, he would have missed the exact moment she recognized him. There was a barely perceptible hesitation in her step and then she was coming toward him again, her stride graceful, her lovely face smoothed free of any discernible expression.

He rose as she neared and held out his hand. With Abigail and David in the room, he had intended not to mention the night before, but she apparently had no such reservations.

She extended her hand, her demeanor gracious, patrician, coolly cordial. "Hello, I'm

Joanna Damaron, and I believe we met last night in the Caldwells' garden."

"Yes, we did." As he had the night before, he held her hand longer than he should, taking the opportunity to study her closely. She had the famous Damaron silver mark, all right. Her streak was a half inch wide and ran straight back from her hairline above her right eyebrow. The streak was simply a paler shade of her hair, and last night the moonlight had washed out the color so that he hadn't been able to see it. If he had he might have made the connection. Then again probably not. It would have never occurred to him that a woman who could melt against him and moan so sweetly would be engaged.

She withdrew her hand. "I assume you were heading up the party's security?"

"That's right."

A brief smile touched her lips. "Well, you did say that you weren't a guest."

The anger came at him again, surging into his throat, threatening to choke him. Damn her, she was acting as if nothing out of the ordinary had happened between them. As if she had been totally unaffected. "Yes, I did say that. But you"—he paused to allow his gaze to rake over her with deliberate insolence—"didn't mention that you were about to be married."

Something flashed in her eyes, but then quickly vanished. "Didn't I?"

"Trust me, I would have remembered." He glanced down at her left hand and saw a large pear-shaped solitaire sparkling there. "I would have also remembered an engagement ring that large."

"I wasn't wearing it when I met you. My fiancé presented the ring to me last night at the end of the party."

"It was quite romantic," Abigail volunteered. "Brett planned it as a surprise to Joanna, didn't he, darling?"

"Yes." She broke eye contact with Cale and moved past him to a chair.

"But then this whole engagement has been rather a whirlwind event," Abigail continued in explanation to Cale. "They've known each other for years, but suddenly they upped and surprised all of us with their announcement and insisted that the wedding take place as soon as possible. That was just a few days ago and now the wedding is only two short weeks away. It's all been very exciting." She glanced at her niece, her expression briefly unreadable. "But then Joanna has always known her own mind."

Jo smiled at her aunt. "I'm sure Mr. Whitfield would like to get down to business. He must be a very busy man."

He dropped back into his own chair and leveled a fixed gaze on her. "You called me Cale last night."

A faint flush crept beneath her pale beige skin, but her response came easily. "That's right. How could I have forgotten?"

She hadn't, he thought. If there was one thing he *was* sure of, he had gotten to her when they had kissed in the garden. She was like ice today but last night she had been warm and pliable.

As if she knew what he was thinking she cleared her throat. "Now, my wedding shouldn't prove that difficult or complicated for you. You can—"

"When it comes to protecting your family, I'm sure you wouldn't want me to do a half-baked job."

He had the distinct impression that she would have been gritting her teeth if her features weren't schooled to such a perfect calm. "No, of course not. I'm only saying that it should all be straightforward for you. We'll provide you with a guest list, of course, but you could probably turn this whole affair over to one of your men."

She didn't want him anywhere around. Perversely the knowledge made him feel much better.

"Darling," Abigail said, addressing her niece. "Cale's uncle has provided our security for years and always took care of us personally. I'm sure Raymond has made Cale aware of the people he'll be protecting. Royalty, statesmen, the President may even come. This may be a hurried-up affair but your wedding will be one to remember and we need the additional security."

Jo inhaled a deep breath, then exhaled it slowly. "I understand that, Aunt Abigail. But *because* Raymond Whitfield has provided our security for years, he should have it down to a science. He probably even has a blueprint in his files outlining Damaron events. He's already overseen the magnetic scan on the invitations. The rest should be fairly easy—"

"I don't do any job on automatic pilot, Jo." His voice was soft but it drew the attention of the two other occupants of the room.

She stared back at him for a moment, then lightly shrugged. "All right then. As Aunt Abigail said, the wedding is being arranged quickly and—"

"Any particular reason for that?"

All traces of silver in her eyes vanished as they turned pure green. He almost smiled. She obviously hadn't liked his question, and he couldn't blame her. The question was completely out of line but he hadn't been able to stop himself. He hated the cool, composed facade she was presenting to him, and he was finding he preferred her annoyance to her indifference.

"Why do you ask?"

"For the job I need to do, the more time there is to plan, the better."

She paused, carefully formulating her answer before she spoke again. "Once my fiancé and I decided to marry we saw no reason to wait. If that causes you any problems, I apologize. But rest assured that on any matter other than the wedding date you'll have a completely free rein."

"That's good to hear. Then you won't object if I move into one of your guest houses for the duration. Abigail, I assume you will make one available as you have in the past?"

"Certainly. David will see to it, won't you, David?"

"Consider it done."

"Good," she said, smiling broadly. "And an excellent idea, too, Cale."

"It's a terrible idea," Jo countered. "Why on earth would you need to move onto the grounds?"

Ah. At last a response that wasn't so damned controlled. More than anything at this moment he wanted to touch her, to kiss her, to break through to her as he had last night. But that was impossible now. She was about to become a married woman, and he needed to remember it.

"Your wedding is going to require day by day supervision, Jo." Despite the minilecture he had just given himself, he deliberately said her name, enjoying the fact that the familiarity seemed to bother her. "Your wedding gifts will have to be screened and everyone who comes onto the grounds, whether they're simply delivery personnel or workers who will be setting up for the event, will have to be overseen and cleared."

"All right, but that's during the day. Why do you have to be here at night?"

His smile broadened. "All kinds of things happen at night—you just never know."

Abigail gestured to Jo with her cigarette holder. "He's absolutely right." Jo remained quiet. "Darling, you know the need for enhanced security as well as I do. Jonah had to handle an incident just the other day." To Cale, she said, "Jonah Damaron. He's in Paris at the moment. Besides, Joanna, you know as well as I do that special events draw out very strange people."

"If you decide to go with someone else for the job, I'll certainly understand." He wanted the job. He needed it to establish himself in this section of the country. Granted his uncle's name and endorsement would go a long way to recommend him, but a Damaron event under his belt would establish him. If they passed on him, it would make it ten times harder for him to gain a foothold.

So why had he offered to withdraw? Simple. Because he had wanted to see how Jo would react. How unprofessional was that? he asked himself grimly.

Abigail spoke up. "I see no problem with letting Cale do things his way, do you, Joanna? Anyone else we would hire would have the same stipulation."

"Yes, of course. You're right." Jo looked at him. "You'll have carte blanche. Whatever you need, just ask."

With a smile he hoped portrayed nothing more than professionalism, he stood. "Thank you. I'll move in this evening and get started."

The enigmatic David opened the door for him, but before Cale left, he cast a last look at Jo. "Don't worry. I'll do everything I can to make sure your wedding comes off as smoothly as possible. Abigail, it was a pleasure meeting you."

"You, too, Cale. It'll be lovely having you around." Abigail waited until David had shut the door after him before she turned to her great-niece. "All right, my darling, let's have it. What happened between you two last night?"

"Nothing."

"Nothing?"

"Almost nothing," Jo clarified. Gazing down at the diamond on her finger, she absently twisted it back and forth so that it caught the light.

"David, do you believe that?"

He sent Jo a smile of conspiracy. "I always believe her."

"Thank you, David."

The cigarette holder sliced through the air. "Bah! You're both telling me stories, which is not at all kind of you. Joanna, tell me about the *almost* nothing."

She surged to her feet. "There's nothing to tell."

"Really?" Abigail examined her nails. "With the tension between you two as thick as it was, I would have expected something extremely interesting. But I'm pleased, really pleased, that I was wrong, and it's not a thing more than what I would expect of you. Being engaged you would never consider behaving inappropriately."

Jo rolled her eyes at David, who chuckled. Damarons behaved appropriately only when it suited them, as Abigail well knew. Her aunt was baiting her, pure and simple, and any other time Jo would have engaged in a teasing match. But not today. "Have you seen Kylie this morning?"

"I don't think she's down yet. David?"

"Haven't seen her, but I'll go check on her if you like."

"Thanks anyway, but I'll go up. I intended to anyway."

He moved toward the door. "Then I'm

outta here. I've got a date at the club to play tennis."

"Have a good time," Jo called to his departing back. He raised a hand in response.

Abigail frowned, her concentration elsewhere. "Kylie should be up and helping you with your wedding."

"She will be. I spoke with the doctor about her. He said she simply needs to rest. If she's not better soon, I'll take her in for a blood test to see if she's anemic, but I don't think that will be necessary. She's more than likely picked up a little virus." Guilt nipped at her conscience. She had indeed spoken with the doctor about Kylie—a defensive move on her part—but she'd only told the doctor Kylie's symptoms, not the cause. "Besides I've got all the help I need for the wedding."

"Still—"

"I'll go see if she's up yet." She started out of the room, but her aunt's voice stopped her.

"Are you sure there's nothing you'd like to tell me about Cale?"

Jo smiled wryly. "I'm positive. As usual you're letting your imagination run wild."

Abigail snorted inelegantly. "Imagination has very little to do with it, my darling. All I had to do was open my eyes."

"Perhaps you need glasses," Jo said, her tone light.

"Not on your longest day will I ever need glasses."

"Whatever you say, Aunt Abigail."

"Exactly." Abigail watched as her great-niece left the room, then opened a drawer beside her and pulled out her address book and a pair of reading glasses. With the reading glasses perched on her nose, she thumbed through the address book until she found the number she was seeking, then dialed and waited until the phone on the other end was answered. "Raymond? Abigail. Now tell me some more about this nephew of yours and don't leave out a thing."

Quietly Jo slipped into her sister's room. The drapes were half drawn, casting shadows across the floor. "Kylie?" she said softly.

"I'm over here."

She had to move farther into the room before she was able to spot her sister, where she sat on the window seat, partially hidden by the drapes, still in her nightgown. With her knees drawn up to her chest, her baby-fine hair uncombed, and her blue eyes shadowed, she looked much younger than her eighteen years. "Good, you're up."

The smile Jo forced to her face was lost on Kylie.

She didn't turn, but kept staring out the

window, down at the drive that circled in front of the house. "Who is he?"

Jo walked over to see who her sister was looking at and saw Cale, standing down on the drive, gazing toward the landscaped grounds to his right and the meadow beyond. His brown hair gleamed in the sunlight and even from the height of the second-story window, she could see the assurance that defined him and the sensuality that hit her so hard, she couldn't breathe. She'd seen it during their meeting this morning and in the garden last night when he'd come upon her.

She'd been feeling vulnerable and alone. Her defenses had been down. And in that one unguarded moment she'd allowed him to slip beneath them. In the moonlight he had seemed nonthreatening. He'd told her he didn't want anything from her. But even so, she couldn't explain her response to him. Fortunately she'd come to her senses and run away.

If she hadn't, the enormity of her mistake would have been incalculable. She was an engaged woman, and he'd been nothing more than a stranger. She had been incredibly stupid to give in to the urge to go with his kisses and let herself feel his heat.

She'd like nothing more than to forget last night, but his anger with her this morning had been palpable, at least to her. And she was almost positive that he wasn't going to let her off easily.

"Jo?"

Her sister's voice refocused her attention. "His name is Cale Whitfield. He's going to be in charge of the security at the wedding."

"I thought he might be a policeman." Kylie's voice was dull, tired.

"No, he's taken over his uncle's security firm—that's all." She threw one last glance out the window at Cale. His stance was alert, his gaze searching. Obviously he wasn't a man who missed much. She was going to have to be extremely careful of him.

She reached out and gently combed her fingers through Kylie's flaxen-blond hair with its delicate silver streak. "How are you feeling this morning?"

"I didn't sleep much last night."

"Why didn't you come to my room? We could have raided the kitchen and then watched an old movie together like we've always done when you've had trouble sleeping."

"You needed your rest. Besides, I wasn't hungry."

"When's the last time you've eaten?"

"I eat."

Jo gazed worriedly at her sister, trying to gauge the extent of her recent weight loss. She'd been eleven when Kylie had been born, and with one look at her new baby sister she had lost her heart to her. From that moment on she had been her sister's protector and champion. Kylie had been an angelic baby, a fairy child, filled with laughter, brimming over with love. When five years later their parents had been killed in a plane crash, some of Kylie's laughter had died. Of course she had been deeply affected, too, but she'd done her best to push her feelings aside and intensify and expand her role of looking out for her sister.

"You need to get out of this room, sweetheart. Your friends are calling and coming by."

"I've talked to one or two and told them I don't feel well." Kylie rose to move restlessly around the room.

"That's an okay excuse for a few days, but that reason is not going to keep them satisfied for long. Besides, you're not going to feel any better as long as you stay cooped up in here. Come on, honey," she said, gently cajoling. "Get dressed and run around with me today. I need your help with the wedding."

For the first time Kylie glanced at her. "Jo, you could organize a presidential inaugural, including all the balls and entertainment events with one hand tied behind your back and both eyes closed."

Jo chuckled. "First of all, I couldn't. And secondly this isn't an inaugural coming up. It's my wedding."

Kylie chewed on an already ragged fingernail. "I-I know I'm not acting like it, but I'm happy for you. Brett seems to be a good man."

Jo went to her and gently pulled her finger from her mouth. "If you chew on that any longer, you're going to draw blood. And you're changing the subject. I still need help."

"Doing what?"

"Well"—she searched her mind—"for all sorts of things. For instance invitations—"

"Those went out two days ago. They've all been hand-delivered."

"How do you know that?"

"Abigail told me."

"Right," she said, mentally shifting to another tactic. "But I'm worried that I may have forgotten some people. I need to double-check the guest list, plus a million other details that I can't think of offhand. *Plus*—and this is a *big* plus—I need you to come over to the studio and help me brainstorm ideas for your dress. We don't have much time, and my maid of honor needs a very special dress."

Kylie's mouth twisted with a faint touch of humor. "Now I know you've gone over the edge. No one has helped you with any of your designs since the first doll dress you made when you were seven years old."

"Six and that's beside the point. You need to get out of this room."

"No." Kylie picked up a book, put it back

down, picked it up again, then dropped it. "Oh, Jo, I'm so miserable and worried"—her voice broke—"and this room is the only place where I feel safe."

"I know, honey." Jo went to her and took her into her arms, hugging her. "But haven't I always taken care of you?" she asked in a whisper. "I will this time too."

Kylie pulled away, her blue eyes stark with fear. "Yes, but this isn't like I fell down and scraped my knee. It's not a normal, everyday—"

"Shhh." She framed Kylie's face with her hands. "I've always taken care of you and I'm not going to stop now. Trust me. We're going to get through this together."

Cale stood on the porch of the guest house, gazing out at the night. David had been waiting for him when he'd arrived a couple of hours before and with a minimum of conversation had shown him to where he would be living the next two weeks.

He had found a refrigerator stocked with staples, a large bowl of fruit gracing the kitchen counter, and several vases of fresh flowers scattered throughout the four large rooms of the two-bedroom guest house. It was a very livable combination of comfort, convenience, and luxury. Everything he could possibly want.

In fact he should be inside right now, drawing up a plan to ensure that Jo's wedding would go off without a hitch in the security. But instead he was spending his time on the porch, gazing up toward the mansion where he assumed Jo and her family were having dinner.

He wondered if Jo's fiancé was having dinner with them. He hadn't seen anyone arrive, but then the guest house was located at the rear of the main house, some distance away. By tomorrow he'd know the names of everyone who stepped foot on the estate, but for tonight he was left to wonder.

Damn it all, who was the guy, anyway? The guy who'd won the hand of the fair Jo and would be married to her in two weeks. Successful, cultivated, sophisticated were just a few of the traits that would be a given with Jo's fiancé. By tomorrow night he'd damned well know the rest.

He was a fool for insisting on doing this job himself. A total fool. He could have just as easily overseen everything from the office. But he'd told the truth when he'd said he did no job on automatic. And there was also another truth, a strong truth that could not be denied.

He couldn't get the night before out of his mind. How could she have kissed him the way she had and the next day coolly hire him for her wedding that was to take place in two weeks?

Had last night been some sort of game for her? Using him to get some final kicks before she married? But if that were the case, surely she would have gone after more than kisses. God knows he would have been willing.

His fist slammed against one of the porch's supporting pillars. He wanted an explanation, and he would damn well get one.

Damn her for being so unforgettable.

Damn her for kissing him when she belonged to someone else.

But most of all, damn *him* for wanting more of her kisses, more of her.

TWO

The morning was still. Only feathery traces of dawn-pink remained in a sky that was turning bluer by the minute. Cale walked over the meticulously kept grounds that immediately surrounded the house, beginning to familiarize himself with every tree, every shrub, every dip in the ground, however slight. The process would make it easier for him in the days ahead to notice anything out of order. Later, he would tour the estate's entire three hundred acres but for now the house and the few acres surrounding it were his first concern.

He heard a splash of water somewhere off to his left and instinctively turned toward it. The sound came from an area he hadn't explored yet and as he drew nearer he heard more sounds of water.

Preferring to approach the area indirectly,

he threaded his way through a thicket of tall shrubbery and stopped just before he cleared it.

A long, rectangular swimming pool lay before him. The water sparkled with glints as the sun rose slowly in the sky. A woman swam back and forth across the pool, her strokes clean and strong.

It was Jo, of course. Jo, with her controlled movements and perfect body and features, looking every inch the goddess he had initially thought she might be—an ice goddess who had melted in his arms in the warm silvery moonlight.

He left the concealment of the shrubs and strolled over to the edge of the pool, enjoying the sight of watching her swim toward him. Just for a moment he allowed himself to fantasize that she knew he was there and that she was in fact swimming to him, only him.

But she was a Damaron, which by definition meant she moved and lived on a rarefied plane, populated only by other Damarons and those they deemed worthy to join them. He was simply the hired help. To top it off, she was an engaged woman about to be another man's wife. Everything about her signaled, *Stop. Don't go any further.*

And he wouldn't. He simply wanted to talk to her.

Her hand grasped the edge of the pool as she finished her last lap. Emerging from the water, she climbed the pool steps, her limbs gleaming with moisture and the morning sun, her hair wet and slicked back.

Then she saw him and came to an abrupt stop on the top step, her eyes wide and wary. "What are you doing here?"

Holding her gaze with his, he silently reached down for her hand and drew her up the last step and out of the pool. There was a thick towel folded on the end of a chaise lounge. He handed it to her.

She held the towel against herself as if it were a shield. "I asked what you're doing here."

"I heard you." Without even trying she pushed all his buttons. No question, he was going to have to get a grip on these wayward feelings he was having about her. He smiled slowly. "I was just surprised you'd forgotten, that's all."

"Forgotten what?"

"I'm living here now—remember?"

She'd remembered all right. Last night before she had gone to bed she had gazed out her window toward the distant guest house. His lights had been on, and she had wondered what he was doing. In fact, she'd stood by the window for an extraordinarily long time, thinking and wondering about him. In the end she had gone to bed deeply troubled. "I meant, what are you doing down here by the pool. You're not dressed for a swim."

Her poise grated on his nerves. He could still taste her, while she seemed bent on forgetting anything ever happened between them. It made him want to lash out and verbally claw at her. "I could be," he said softly. "Say the word and I could be undressed in two seconds flat and in the pool with you. Or the bushes. Or wherever."

He studied the faint flush that crept upward from her neck with satisfaction. He took the sight as an affirmation that what had happened in the garden had been real. She was as affected by him as he was by her. The fiery chemistry of the night before hadn't been a figment of his imagination. Of course the knowledge didn't justify his crudeness.

But he *felt* and he wanted her to feel. And in some vague, indeterminate way, he *hurt* and he wanted her to hurt too.

So much for getting a grip on his feelings.

He scanned the white one-piece suit she was wearing. "Naturally you'd have to get undressed too. *More* undressed than you are now."

She wasn't used to being on the defensive with anyone, but with Cale there seemed no other way. "I'm not undressed in any way, shape, or form."

He nodded his agreement. "Only in my mind."

He'd just managed to agree with her and thoroughly disconcert her at the same time. Neat trick, Jo reflected ruefully.

"Don't you ever wear any other color but white?" he asked, his voice turning unexpectedly gruff. She looked glorious in it, her chest rising and falling from the exertion of her swim, her breasts mounding above the low neckline of the swimsuit.

And she wasn't his. He had to remember that. He also had to remember that she was his employer.

"White isn't a color." She leaned over from the waist and twisted her long hair into a single rope, wringing it free of water.

Within seconds she could irritate and arouse, two primal yet opposite responses. She was like no other woman he had ever known. And all his warnings and reminders to himself weren't helping worth a damn. "Then why don't you wear a color, *any* color, *pick* a color."

She straightened and directed a level gaze at him. "Is this really about the color or rather the *lack* of color I choose to wear?"

No it wasn't. Worse, he didn't know what it was about. "It can be about anything you'd like. What would you like to talk about?"

"Nothing. I'd like to talk about *nothing*. One of the things I've always enjoyed about early mornings is the silence and the fact that no one else is around." She wrapped her hair with the towel he had handed her, then reached for another to wipe herself down. And she waited, waited to see what he would do or say next. She didn't have to wait long.

"Do you often come down here to swim at this time of day?"

She propped a foot against the chaise lounge and leaned over to towel off the length of one shapely leg, then the other. "What I do or don't do really isn't any of your business."

She was the ice goddess again, and he couldn't stand it. His hands closed around her upper arms and brought her upright. "You're wrong, Jo. You're very *much* my business. You're the centerpiece in this upcoming wedding. That means your family and all the guests will be revolving around *you*. It's my job to keep an eye on you, and I'm committed to doing an excellent job."

She wrenched free of his grasp. "That sounds strangely like a threat."

"I never threaten, Jo."

The dark intensity of his eyes startled her. In fact, *he* startled her, every time she saw him, though she didn't know why. Maybe it had something to do with his chemical makeup. Every cell, every fiber, every drop of blood, and every millimeter of bone in him combined to form a man who had a powerful effect on

the world around him. He couldn't walk into a
moonlit garden without disturbing its peace.
He couldn't sit in her aunt's sunroom without
making the air electric. He couldn't come upon
her in the stillness of the early morning without stirring up her emotions and sending them
swirling. His very presence impacted on everything that was in her, demanding a response.

And he was the *absolutely* wrong man at the
absolutely wrong time.

"You're overqualified for this job, Cale.
You're used to guarding presidents. I'm just a
bride."

"Not yet you're not," he drawled. It had
been a stupid thing for him to say, but it had an
interesting effect on her. He watched emotion
shift in and out of her eyes. Annoyance. Anger.
Fear? No, it couldn't have been fear. He very
much needed to get a grip. "Obviously,
though, if things stay on schedule you will be a
bride. But not *just* a bride. You'll be a Damaron
bride, which means—"

She sighed, fully aware of the baggage that
came with her family name. "Point taken.
Never mind."

He broke eye contact with her. Just walk
away, he told himself. Just walk away. He
looked back at her. "And there's another reason why I need to be on this job," he said. "You
kissed me in the Caldwells' garden."

"So?" She gave an elegant shrug. "Unless

those were the first kisses you've ever received,
I can't imagine why you would take them so
seriously."

"You were there, Jo. You tell me."

"That's what I'm trying to do. That whole
encounter was a mistake. *My* mistake and I
apologize."

Anger flashed through him, the now-famil-
iar anger that had been with him since yesterday morning when he had learned it would be
her wedding for which he would be providing
security. He attempted to bank the anger
down. "I don't want an apology," he said as
calmly as he could manage. "I want an explanation. Why would an engaged woman kiss a
man she had just met?"

She wished her answers were as good as his
questions. She also wished she'd never given in
to the inexplicable urge to kiss him. Lord help
her, she hadn't been able to get the kisses or
him out of her mind. "And why would you
choose to make such a big deal out of what was
essentially nothing more than a few simple
kisses?" She turned away to put on her white
terry-cloth robe.

Damn. Just when he thought he might have
a chance to walk away without completely losing his cool, she had to go and say something
like that. Without giving her a chance to don
the robe, he turned her back to him. "There

wasn't a damn thing simple about those kisses
and you know it."

"Really?" She schooled her expression to
one of vague curiosity. "You mean you thought
they *weren't* simple?"

Her implication that any other interpreta-
tion on his part was extremely odd only added
fuel to the fire of anger growing in his gut.
How could they have experienced the same
thing, yet had such vastly different responses?
"I *know* they weren't, lady. I've had all kinds of
kisses in my life, and I know when kisses mean
something."

She just bet he had had all kinds of kisses.
And that he'd given many more than he'd received. She had only to look at his mouth to
see the sensuality etched there. She had only to
remember how he had kissed her. And how she
had responded. "It was a chance encounter that
never should have happened."

"But it did, Jo, and there had to be a reason. Dammit, you're *engaged*."

A faint frown appeared across her brow.
"Quit trying to make this so complicated, Cale.
It's not. True it happened and we can't change
it. I've said it was my mistake. I've apologized.
The matter is closed."

His eyes narrowed. "I don't think so."

Something in his look made her shiver.
"I'm cold," she said, and reached for her robe.
This time he let her put it on, but before

she could belt it around her, he drew her
against him.

She gasped at the contact of his hard, muscled body. "Don't—I'll get you wet."

"Get me wet," he ground out. "And while
you're at it, let's exchange a few more of those
simple kisses. If they're so damned simple, there
should be no problem."

Before she could speak, his mouth came
down on hers with a fierceness that took her
breath away. Where the kisses in the garden
had been soft and melting, this kiss was hard
and fiery, like a powerful blast from a furnace.
He kissed her with a shattering power and
mastery. He made no compromises as he drove
his tongue deep into her mouth. The kiss was
about possession, pure and simple. About sex.
About control. And there was nothing she
could do but to go along with it, because she
couldn't stop the instant response that flamed
in her veins, in her loins, in her brain. She
could only hold on to him and comply with his
demands.

His hand slid beneath the robe, around the
back of her waist and then down to her hips
and the rounded curves of her bottom. He
pulled her against him until she could feel his
male hardness against her lower stomach
through the thin, damp material of her swimsuit. His actions were unabashedly carnal and
sexual. He wasn't hiding his need from her. He

wasn't playing a game. In the most basic of ways he was showing her he wanted her. And God help her, she wanted him.

There was nothing simple about this kiss, just as there had been nothing simple about the kisses in the garden. What was she going to do?

His heat seeped into her skin, infusing her with desire and need. His masculinity was like dynamite, threatening to explode with dangerous power if she allowed it.

Acknowledging the immediate need to end the kiss, she did the opposite, wrapping her arms tightly around him and sinking against him, making it even easier for him to mold her to him.

He kissed her time and again as his restless hands moved over her. He wasn't using force with her, but rather desire, sweet and thick, sending it flowing through her veins like heated honey. He demanded and she gave. There didn't seem to be anything else she could do. But then as if he weren't satisfied, his fingers drove upward beneath the back of one leg of her swimsuit until he could take hold of her rounded buttock. He kneaded and stroked her soft skin and pulled her even closer against him.

He was making her feel too much, *want* too much, she thought hazily. If he didn't stop kissing her soon, there would be no turning back. Desperately she tried to find even a thin strand of control, but how could she stop something that felt so good, so right? Fortunately, unfortunately, he slowly broke off the kiss and eased away from her, leaving her feeling bereft, shaken, and completely confused.

"You're not cold," he said harshly, gazing down at her, heat sparking in the depths of his brown eyes. "That's the damned problem. On the outside you *look* cold, but on the inside you're pure fire. The question is, does your fiancé know about the fire?"

"My fiancé?"

He grinned with wolfish satisfaction. "What's the matter? Did my *simple* kisses drive him right out of your mind?"

Gathering her strength as best she could, she pressed her hands against his chest and pushed away from him, but he released her before she was ready and she nearly fell. His hand shot out to steady her until she could stand on her own. "You shouldn't have done that," she said, tying the belt of her robe around her waist with shaking hands.

"Impossible," he said softly. "It's all impossible. It was impossible for me *not* to do that. I touch you, I kiss you, and I'm lost. It's the damnedest thing. I can't seem to get enough of the way you respond to me. But I know—you and me, *we're* impossible. I do know that. And the really damnable thing is that I want nothing more than to make us possible."

"You can't."

"You're not listening to me." He lifted a hand and lightly touched her cheek. "I said I *know* I can't, *shouldn't,* but I can't stop myself. Hell, don't you think I wish I could?"

"Cale—"

"What?" He bit the word out in frustration. "You're engaged? I know that. All we've done is kiss? I know that too. So can you tell me something I don't know? Like why I've met you too late?"

"No," she said softly. "No, I can't."

"Then can you tell me what we can do about this? So that I'm not angry all the time? So that I'll back away from you and not mind it a bit?"

She shook her head.

"No, I know you can't. Because we're not talking moral or immoral here, Jo. We're talking about a force of nature that I can't explain. But I've had to face it. When will you?" He paused and drew in a ragged breath. "Because, Jo, I know I'm not feeling these things alone. I *know* I'm not."

No, he wasn't. No way was he alone. And if things were different she'd probably go straight back into his arms. But things *weren't* different. Her hand fluttered outward toward him, but when she realized what she'd done she pulled it back. "Okay, okay—to a certain extent you're right."

"To a certain extent?" He gave a bark of disbelief.

"All I can tell you is that we've got to stop. I'm about to be married."

"Right. You got a multicarat rock on your finger. The wedding date has been set and the invitations have been sent out. But none of that means a damned thing when compared to the chemistry we have between us."

"The chemistry will fade."

"I don't think it will, and it's driving me straight around the bend. It doesn't make sense, but there it is."

She had no defense against him. She couldn't even bring herself to argue. What he said was true. Under the circumstances her response to him had been scandalous. How could she blame him? He had only initiated the kiss. She had been the one who had acquiesced, caught fire, and responded. The only reason they still weren't kissing was because he had drawn away. Not her.

And even now the fierce fire she saw burning in his eyes was almost her undoing. She swallowed against a lump that had formed in her throat. "I could fire you, you know. And then you wouldn't have to stay around here, around me."

"So are you going to? Fire me?"

"I might. I'll have to think about it."

All she'd have to do was say the word and he'd be gone, and then one of her problems would be solved. But the reality was he was more than a mere problem. He'd been right. As amazing as it seemed, there were forces of nature involved and every time she thought about firing him, she couldn't bring herself to do it. She wanted him around. She wanted him to kiss her again. She was pitiful, she thought ruefully. Really pitiful. Why had he shown up now in her life?

She said no more. His jaw clenched and unclenched. "Just tell me one thing, Jo. Why are you getting married in two weeks?"

She threw up her hands. "Good heavens, Cale. Why does anyone get married?"

"I'm not interested in anyone else's reasons —just yours."

"My reasons are none of your business."

"No, you're right. They're not. But tell me anyway."

His voice was husky, beguiling, bewildered. She felt herself shaking, aching to go back in his arms.

"See, Jo, you didn't warn me that you belonged to someone else that night we met. I kissed you and you kissed me back and, baby, you got me hook, line, and sinker. You made me want you and now I can't stop. Worse, I don't even want to stop."

"Cale, listen to me. I take full responsibility for what happened. I should never have allowed those kisses. But they happened. And now you've got to forget them."

"As easy as that? And how about what just happened between us? You want me to forget that too? Can *you*?"

"I will. And you need to too. You have a job to do and I won't interfere with it, but you've got to leave me alone. You've got to—"

He groaned, and the sound carried real pain. "I tried, but my good intentions and common sense didn't last longer than a few minutes when faced with you. Jo, listen to me. I'm a man who plans for all contingencies, but there was no way I could plan for you. That night in the Caldwells' garden was like a blow between the eyes for me, and I haven't been able to recover. Yeah, all we've done is kiss, but then that's what makes what's happening between us so remarkable."

She wanted to cry, for him, for her, for the ache in her heart. "I'm so sorry, Cale. I'm so sorry."

"*Joanna!*"

Cale turned and glanced over his shoulder to see a tall, slim man, expensively dressed and with perfect bearing, striding toward them. "Anyone you know?"

She looked, then drew her fingertips across

her brow in an unconsciously soothing gesture. "It's Brett. My fiancé."

"Wonderful," he muttered. "Just wonderful. But then I've been looking forward to meeting him."

"Please go."

He felt wounded, raw, and each look from her, each word, made the pain that much worse. "I wouldn't miss meeting him for the world."

They hadn't come to either a resolution or a solution, but for the moment she couldn't think of a thing in the world to do about it. For the benefit of the man coming toward her, she had no choice but to plaster a smile on her face. "Good morning, Brett."

"Good morning, darling." Brett bent to press a tender kiss on her cheek.

And watching, Cale had to restrain himself from tearing the man's arms out of his sockets. He didn't know what he would have done if Brett had kissed Jo on her lips, the lips he had just kissed so thoroughly. God help him, the next two weeks were going to be hell, he thought. Pure hell.

Brett turned to him, a slightly puzzled expression on his good-looking face. "I'm Brett Saunders."

Pulling himself together, Cale shook his hand. "I'm Cale Whitfield. My firm has been hired to be in charge of the security for the wedding."

Brett's expression cleared. "Of course. Raymond Whitfield's nephew. That's great. He gave you the highest recommendation."

"That's what I hear."

A portion of his puzzlement returned. "So you were talking with Joanna about the wedding plans?"

Jo cleared her throat. "Yes—"

"No," Cale said, deliberately cutting her off. "I was exploring the grounds, heard water splashing and came to investigate."

"That's good. I'm glad you're on top of things. Unfortunately, since we're having the wedding so quickly, problems are going to crop up. And because of my work I have to leave most of the wedding plans to Joanna, and now I know I can leave the security to you."

Brett slid his hand around Jo's waist and drew her against his side. Cale's gaze sharpened. Did he imagine it, or had Jo stiffened? No. More than likely he had seen what he wanted to see. "Rest assured you can leave everything safely in my hands."

Had the double entendre been deliberate? Jo wasn't sure. But then it didn't matter, because Brett hadn't seemed to notice. She attempted to take charge of the conversation. "What are you doing here so early, Brett?"

He chuckled and gave her a quick squeeze.

"I wanted to see my soon-to-be bride before I went off to work this morning. Thought we might have breakfast together."

"Sounds wonderful," she assured him, not daring to glance at Cale.

"I was hoping you'd say that. I'm going to have to be putting in some long hours in the next ten days. I hate it, but it's the only way I'll be able to take time off for that honeymoon of ours."

Even the *thought* of Jo off on a honeymoon with this man—hell, *any* man—made bile rise in Cale's throat. "Does that mean you won't be around here much?"

"I'll be here as often as I can. I'll just have to see how each day goes." Speculation entered Brett's eyes. "Why do you ask?"

"I'm going to be setting up a security post at the gate, but I'll make certain you can get in anytime."

Brett relaxed. "I'd appreciate that." He reached for her left hand. "Where's your ring, darling?"

"I didn't want to swim, wearing it."

"That's probably a good idea, even though I doubt if a few chemicals would hurt *that* diamond." He laughed as if he thought he'd said something funny. "Come on, Joanna. Let's go see what the cook has made for breakfast."

"Did you call ahead and tell her you were coming?"

"Yes."

"Then she's probably made your favorite pecan waffles."

Brett laughed again. "Which is exactly why I called ahead. See you later, Cale. Oh, and if you have any problems, notify me. Joanna will give you the number."

"Thank you."

Cale watched Jo walk off arm in arm with Brett. The man had turned out to be exactly the type he had guessed she would marry. From his Italian-designer suit to his manicured nails, Brett was urbane and sophisticated and no doubt extremely wealthy.

Cale didn't like him. No surprise there. The man could be the pope, and Cale still wouldn't want to like or trust him.

He and Jo had kissed. They hadn't vowed eternal love for each other. But he couldn't shake the feeling that he wouldn't be able to stand it if he didn't have her at least once.

Impossible. The whole damned thing was impossible.

THREE

Cale had left her alone for over twenty-four hours, Jo reflected, reaching for the phone and punching in a series of numbers. She'd caught glimpses of him as he went about his work, but he had made no move to approach her. The fact that he hadn't should have made her feel better, more secure. Instead she was decidedly jumpy. Their last encounter had been too charged, too volatile, for her to believe he was simply going to forget all the words and emotions that lay between them.

How could she expect him to do something that she couldn't do herself?

But she must. Nothing more could happen between them. Unfortunately on top of all the other pressure she was under, his presence and the heated way he made her feel was overloading her nerves.

She had to stop letting him get to her. And she had to stop allowing him to take her attention away from Brett and Kylie. *They* were the important people in her life.

She frowned as she realized the phone was still ringing. She was about to hang up when she heard her sister answer, her tone desultory.

"Kylie, honey, what were you doing? The phone's been ringing forever."

"Sorry. I guess I didn't hear it."

Jo's frown deepened. Kylie didn't sound one bit better. "Listen, honey. I'm down at the studio, and I need your help."

Kylie sighed. "We talked about this yesterday. You don't need my help."

"And I'm telling you I do. I've narrowed the designs down for your dress to three, and I want you to come make the final choice."

"Jo, your taste is much better than mine."

"But you're going to be wearing the dress, not me."

"Jo—"

Her heart was breaking for her sister, but she felt she had to remain firm. "And I need you for something else too. The wedding consultant is due here in about ten minutes. I can't deal with her alone. I need you for moral support."

"Since when?"

"Since I'm being married in two weeks.

Come on, honey. I'm feeling swamped. I *really* need you."

Kylie was silent for several moments. Finally she said, "I'm not dressed."

"Just throw on anything. It doesn't matter. You could even wear your robe if you absolutely don't want to get dressed. Just come down." Simply getting her out of her room would be a major triumph. "Please, Kylie. I'm desperate. Cut through the east garden. It'll only be a short walk."

More silence, then, "I'm so sorry, Jo. I know I'm letting you down. I don't mean to."

A slight smile touched Jo's lips. The apology was a good sign. In the last week or so Kylie's pain and fear had made her turn inward, become uncharacteristically self-absorbed. The apology had to mean that she was beginning to look outward again. "Forget about me, honey. It's you I'm worried about. You've got to try to pull yourself together. It's important."

"I keep telling myself the same thing, but then I remember what I did . . ."

Jo's hand tightened on the receiver. "I told you that I'm working on the problem."

"I can't get over being scared, Jo." Her voice was a whisper.

"And you won't if you stay in that room. All you do in there is think and remember. So come on down. Please, Kylie, do this for me."

Silence, then, "All right."

"You'll come?"

"I'll try. Yes."

Jo heaved a silent sigh of relief. "Do you want me to come get you so you don't have to walk alone?"

Kylie laughed brokenly. "No, I should at least be able to manage a short walk."

"Okay, then. See you in a few minutes."

Please let her come, she whispered to herself. She hung up the phone and rubbed her forehead. Lord, what was she going to do? Time was running out. She had to think of something . . .

"Good morning."

The sound of Cale's voice made her jerk, sending the three delicate gold bangles on her right arm to jangling. "Good morning," she said, instantly reining in her nerves. How had he gotten in without her hearing him?

Satisfaction secured his smile as he took in the slim cut jeans and pale green silk shirt she had on. "You're wearing color."

Ignoring the comment, she tried to tell herself she hadn't dressed with him in mind this morning. She failed. "Is there something I can do for you?"

To his credit he didn't reply with the obvious, in spite of the opportunity she had inadvertently given him.

"I'm still familiarizing myself with the estate, and since your studio is on the grounds of the estate, I thought I'd drop by and take a look around."

"By all means." She gestured for him to go ahead. She had no intention of interfering with his work. And if she doubted that an inspection of her studio was an integral part of his job she kept quiet. Bigger, more important battles would be coming.

Watching as he explored her world, she took a seat on a high stool in front of one of her drafting tables. Light poured into the large room from windows as tall as the two-story-high ceiling. Spiral stairs reached up to a loft. And everywhere there were portfolios, mounds of fabric samples, and stacks of large drawing tablets.

"So you're a clothing designer?"

"You didn't know?"

He spared her a glance. "I've never kept up with women's fashions, but my uncle mentioned it to me. He said you're quite well known. As a designer, I mean."

"In certain circles."

"Then you're obviously very successful?"

"Yes." Initially the Damaron name had opened doors for her but her own talent and backbreaking hard work had kept the doors wide open for the last eight years.

He picked up a sketch pad and flipped through the pages that held clean-lined drawings of practical, yet sophisticated sportswear and smart, elegant suits. "Do you work here all the time?"

"No." He reminded her of an untamed mountain cat roaming through unfamiliar territory. He looked out of place, and she had to stop herself from flinching every time he touched something of hers. Unreasonably it was as if he were touching her, and unfortunately she remembered all too well how that felt. She didn't want to be reminded. She didn't want to want his touch again. "My office is in New York, but I spend a lot of time here because my sister lives here."

"Sister?" He looked at her. "I haven't met her, have I?"

"I doubt it. Her name is Kylie, and she hasn't been feeling well lately. She rests a lot."

"I need to meet her when she's up to it. I need to be able to recognize her."

He had a way of making his demands seem reasonable. Even the unspoken demands in his kisses. "I'll show you a picture of her."

"Good. Any more family I should know about?"

"Scads. They'll be arriving within the next week or so. I'll have my assistant fax you a list."

"Do those scads include your parents or any more siblings?"

"No, there's just Kylie and me and our cousins. Thirteen years ago my parents, along with four sets of aunts and uncles were killed when their plane crashed in the Alps."

"Of course," he murmured. The news had made a huge splash all over the world, and no one who had heard could likely forget it. He hadn't; he simply hadn't made the connection in his mind between Jo's parents and the crash. "I'm sorry."

She shrugged. "Things happen. It's why the family never flies together anymore. Never." A sad smile touched her lips. "Many times it's awkward and inconvenient, but that's the way it has to be."

He had fully intended to stay away from her. He had felt it would be safer for him to keep plenty of space between them. He was there because he'd simply wanted to see her again, nothing more. But the sadness in her voice undid his intentions and drew him to her side. "It had to have been tough on all of you to have lost a major chunk of your family like that, unexpectedly, without warning, all at once."

"Tough," she said with an agreeing nod, then hesitated, unsure whether she wanted to go any further with the conversation. Even though the facts were public record, the emotions behind them were not. But finally, the unexplainable need for him to understand her, if only a little, made her decide to continue the conversation. Maybe, in some way, in the end, it would keep him from judging her too harshly. "Kylie was only five. I was sixteen. For the most part my cousins were in their late teens, early twenties. But it didn't matter how old we were."

Automatically he finished her thought. "Because suddenly your generation had the responsibility."

She nodded again, looking at him with some surprise. Maybe he *would* be able to understand, at least to a certain extent. "Our youth ended with that plane crash. After that there was no time to be young."

"Except you were still young."

"Yes."

"From the outside looking in you've all done wonderfully."

"We had one another for support, and we've all tried very hard to see that Kylie wouldn't be affected. That she wouldn't lose her childhood." The last was said more to herself than to him.

"How bad could a childhood be with you as a big sister?" he asked softly.

He was serious, she realized. Just for a moment she allowed herself the luxury of envisioning how her life might have been different if she had met him earlier by even a month. But no, she couldn't let herself think about it, not now. "Thank you for saying that. Kylie's always been a sweetheart, easy to love, easy to do for, but there've been times I should have done more."

"I seriously doubt it."

"You don't know."

What was he hearing in her voice? Sadness? "I'd know if you told me. What do you think you should have done for your sister that you didn't do?"

If she told him anything else, she would be making herself even more vulnerable to him than she already was. "Never mind. It was only a casual statement."

"Really? It sounded as if—"

"Really."

He studied her for a moment. "Okay, then, what are you working on now?" he asked, gesturing to the sketches.

Grateful for the change of subject, she said, "Kylie's maid-of-honor dress."

"Pretty," he said, studying the three sketches spread out before her, each one more youthfully elegant than the next.

"Thank you." She smiled. "I guess."

Her smile wound through his knotted insides, warming him. "You guess?"

"You said it yourself." Her smile broadened. "You don't know much about women's fashion."

"I know what I like." His voice was quiet. "I like your sketches, and I like you."

She shook her head. "You *want* me, you

don't like me." Immediately she wished for the words back.

He was silent for a minute while he studied the faint flush that had suddenly appeared on her cheeks. "I wasn't going to go there with this conversation," he finally said in the same quiet voice, "but, okay, I want you. But I also *like* everything I've seen about you so far. Except, of course, for that damn diamond on your hand."

There was nothing threatening in his demeanor or his voice, but she slipped off the stool and moved around the drafting table until she had put its width between them.

He watched her for a moment. "I haven't touched you, you know. I haven't even tried."

He didn't have to, she thought ruefully. All he had to do was enter the same room as her for all her senses to go on alert. "I just wanted to move. Don't read anything else into it."

"Okay—if you say so." He turned his attention back to the designs. "Where's the design for your wedding dress?"

A strange question, but at least it was off the subject of the two of them. "There isn't one."

"Is someone else designing it for you?"

His questions were not only strange, they were sharply intuitive as well. If he was trying to unnerve her, he was succeeding. She glanced out the window to see if she could catch sight of Kylie. Maybe she should have gone up to the house and gotten her after all. "I haven't decided."

"You mean you've chosen designs for your sister, but not for yourself?"

"Yes." She stole a peek at her watch. If Kylie was going to come, she should have been here by now. Should she call again? She was trying everything she could think of to help Kylie, but so far it didn't seem to be enough. Unless she could think of something else, the majority of her hopes were now pinned on Alvin Shaw. She planned to arrange a meeting this afternoon, tomorrow at the latest.

"Jo?"

She hadn't forgotten him—not by a long shot. It was just that all the things that were weighing on her mind tended to collide now and then, distracting her. "I told you Kylie hasn't been feeling well lately. I'm hoping a new dress will lift her spirits."

"She must have several closets full of dresses."

He was right, of course. It had been a slim hope to think that anything as superficial as a new dress would entice Kylie out of her depression. But she was desperate to get her sister back on her feet so they could begin to face what would be coming.

"What is it?" he asked softly.

She blinked. "Excuse me?"

"You had a funny expression on your face just then."

He was so persistent, she wanted to scream. But she couldn't allow herself the indulgence. "You're mistaken. I was thinking about my wedding, that's all."

"Are you pregnant?"

Shock leeched the color from her face. "You are *way* out of line."

"Yeah, you're right. But you never know. It might prove useful for me to know whether I'm guarding one person or two." He paused. "Then again, maybe I'm just plain curious."

She rubbed her forearms, trying to soothe away the feeling that her nerves were going to jump out of her skin at any moment. "Why?"

"Lots of reasons. No reason. Reasons that make sense only to me and a lot that don't."

She knew she shouldn't go one step further with the conversation. She should simply play it safe and stop it where it was. But she couldn't. "For instance?"

"For instance, like no matter how hard I try I can't get you out of my mind. Like . . . I don't want you to be pregnant by that man, *any* man, because I honestly couldn't stand the thought if you were."

She closed her eyes and spoke softly. "I'm not pregnant."

He was silent for a moment, then leaned forward and lightly touched the silver streak in her hair. "Then that must mean you're marrying him because you love him." She didn't say anything. His breath shuddered out. "I want you to know I really *hate* that idea. More than I can say."

She opened her eyes and looked at him. "This is getting us nowhere. Was there something else we needed to discuss?"

"Yes. There's one more thing I need to say. I'm sorry if I'm making this time before your wedding unbearable for you."

The sincerity she heard in his voice shook her almost as much as his kisses had. And she felt terrible knowing he thought he was one hundred percent responsible for her distress. If only they had met under normal circumstances. "If only . . ."

"If only what, Jo?"

She shook her head. "Nothing."

"I'll resign if you want me to," he whispered. "I'll leave."

She was stunned into silence.

His mouth twisted wryly. "It's probably the last time I'll make this offer, so you'd better take me up on it if that's what you really want to do."

"I don't want you to leave." It was a terribly hard admission for her to make, terribly injurious to herself in many ways. And if in that moment he'd made even the tiniest movement toward her, either physically or verbally, she

might have been lost. Thankfully for her he
waited for her to continue. "But perhaps you
could do your job and still manage to stay away
from me."

He shook his head. "That's an unrealistic
hope. I can't ensure your safety and stay away
from you. You're a Damaron, and taking this
job means a lot more than making sure the cer-
emony is not disrupted by some crank."

"It won't be."

"I hope not. But you know much better
than I do that the Damaron family attracts
controversy and emotion like a lightning rod.
Your family is either loved or hated, both col-
lectively and individually. Abigail mentioned
some trouble your cousin Jonah had last week.
And since you brought up your family's plane
crashing in the Alps, I don't think sabotage was
ever ruled out." Color seeped from her face.
"I'm sorry," he said, immediately contrite.
Hurting her was the last thing he wanted to do.

"No, it's okay. You've made your point.
And I've already told you to do whatever you
have to do. It's just that . . ."

"I know," he said, effortlessly taking up her
train of thought. "It's just that what's happening between you and me makes it hard. And
I'm sorry, but I don't have any solution for
that."

She didn't either. Despite everything she'd
said to him and everything she knew, she

wanted nothing more than to go into his arms and have him hold her for a long, long time.

In a remarkably short time she'd gotten used to the way her body softened to fit so exactly and so easily against his. She'd almost become addicted to the scent of his skin, its musky smell that invaded her pores and struck nerves all over her body. She'd come to crave the way his mouth took control of hers and the way his hands moved over her body with such assurance, as if he felt he had the right to do anything to her he chose. And she was very much afraid she loved the way his kisses made her feel, as if there was nothing or no one more important than the two of them. As she stared at him, she felt her arms begin to lift and her body start to sway toward him.

"Excuse me."

She started. If he hadn't reached out and caught her arm to support her, she might have fallen flat on her face in front of the most exclusive society wedding coordinator on the Eastern seaboard.

Jo cleared her throat. "Margaret—I'm sorry. I didn't hear you come in." She eased away from Cale.

Margaret Montgomery, an older woman with considerable savoir faire and a no-nonsense manner waved off her apology. "Don't think a thing about it, Joanna. It's entirely my fault. I probably didn't knock loud enough." Wearing one of her smart trademark hats, this one a vision of tulle and beads, she advanced toward Cale with her hand outstretched. "How do you do? I'm Margaret Montgomery, the consultant for your wedding. And by the way, *congratulations.*"

"Thank you." Cale took her hand with a charm-filled smile Jo had never seen before. But then he'd never had to use a smile to charm her. All he'd had to do was sit down beside her in a garden filled with moonlight and flowers. "It's a pleasure to meet you. I'm Cale Whitfield."

"Whitfield? But I thought—"

Jo spoke up. "Actually, Margaret, Cale is not my fiancé. He's head of security for the wedding."

Margaret who had had years of experience in dealing with all kinds of sensitive situations didn't even blink. "How delightful and quite sensible too. A Damaron wedding must have top-notch security." Brisk and efficient she turned to Jo. "My dear, we don't have a moment to lose. Are you ready to get down to the plans?"

"Yes, I am." She chanced a glance at Cale. Glints of humor sparkled in his eyes. It had obviously been apparent to both Margaret and him what would have happened if the other woman hadn't shown up when she had. "Cale? Would you excuse us please?"

"I'd like to sit in for a while if you don't mind. It's important for me to know as many of the arrangements as possible."

The fact that he was right didn't make it any easier for her to give in to him on that point. He leaned back against a desk, slipped his hands into his slacks' pockets, and crossed his feet at the ankles, irritatingly at ease.

He knew good and well she wouldn't argue with him in front of Margaret. She had already given the woman more than enough to mull over, although she knew Margaret would never betray even the most scarlet of indiscretions. She wouldn't have been able to stay in business as long as she had if she didn't practice discretion as if it were a religion.

Pain shot through her jaw. Lord help her, she was clenching her teeth. She turned her back on Cale and crossed to the drafting table she had been using. "Let's work over here, Margaret." She transferred the sketches there to another table.

"Oh, let me see," the other woman said enthusiastically. "Have you been sketching designs for your bridal gown?"

"*No*. No," she said again, this time without the sharpness in her tone. "Those sketches are for Kylie's dress."

"I can't wait to see your gown. I know it's going to be spectacular, but I don't blame you a bit for wanting to keep it a secret for as long as you can."

Before Cale's questions, she hadn't given a thought to her dress. She glanced at him. Had he guessed something? No, she reassured herself. He couldn't have.

Margaret settled herself on a cushioned stool and laid her notebook on the table. "All right, let's start from the beginning, shall we? I assume the wedding is going to be here on the estate?"

"That's correct."

Margaret leafed through her notebook until she found the appropriate page. "Where exactly?"

Jo ventured another glance at Cale to find him watching her intently. He had the most penetrating eyes she'd ever seen. And dangerous. They could pull a person into their depths and keep a person there, even when a person knew that to stay would be to drown.

"Joanna? Where exactly?"

With effort she pulled her gaze from Cale. "The wedding will take place in the main garden. And in case of rain, there'll be tents, of course." They were the same basic arrangements for any of Abigail's parties that took place in the late spring. She could have recited them in her sleep.

"It will be beautiful, just beautiful." Beaming her approval, Margaret started taking notes with a graceful gold pen. "Now, how many people in your bridal party?"

"Well, besides Kylie . . ." Her mind went blank. "I don't know," she finally had to admit. "I'm not sure."

"No problem," Margaret said brightly. "You can check with your fiancé and get back to me. We'll move on to your colors."

"Colors? I-I haven't made up my mind yet."

Margaret lightly laughed. "I know that I don't have to tell you about colors. They're your business, but with so little time remaining you need to settle these matters as soon as possible."

"Yes, I know. Maybe I'll do spring colors. Or maybe I'll go dramatic—black and white." She gnawed on her bottom lip. "What do you think?"

"*Me*? My dear, it is *your* wedding, *your* day. It should be your decision."

"Yes . . ." On second thought, she reflected, she didn't want Kylie wearing black. Psychologically it would not be a good idea. "I'll go with the spring colors."

"Wonderful." Margaret's voice held approval that a decision had been made. "Now which ones?"

She shrugged. "Blue, lavender, yellow, green, rose."

For one brief moment Margaret's mouth dropped open. "*All* of them?"

She'd merely been listing them, but she said, "Sure, why not."

Margaret fixed a smile on her face. "Not a reason in the world, my dear. If that's what you want, that's what you'll have. Now about the flowers."

Jo gave a negligent wave of her hand. "Anything will do. Whatever you think."

The gold pen stilled. "But what about your bridal bouquet? Most brides have sentimental and very specific ideas about what they want and don't want to carry."

"Whatever is usually carried. I don't know." She glanced at Cale and saw him frowning at her. She tried again. "Something cascading, I guess. Stephanotis, sprays of lilies, and whatever those little orchids are called. You know, the ones that are long and trailing. . . ." She looked back at Cale as if he might give her inspiration. He was still frowning. She shrugged. "A nice mix of several types of flowers will be fine."

Margaret kept the smile firmly fixed on her face. "I tell you what. I'll speak to your florist and have him make several suggestions, and then we'll present them to you."

"Good."

The other woman made a quick notation in

her book then looked at her list. "Now the catering."

"Give it all to Dardinali's. They do our catering."

Margaret's expression turned nonplussed. "But there are decisions you need to make. What would you like them to serve? And do you want a sit-down dinner or a buffet?"

"Just tell them the occasion and leave it to them." She noted that Margaret's baffled expression wasn't changing and silently sighed. She must not be doing a very good job of answering her questions, but she couldn't find it in herself to worry about it.

"And your music?"

"I don't care."

"But surely you know what you'd like to march down the aisle to? These days you don't have to stick to 'The Wedding March.' Canon in D is very popular or 'Jesu Joy of Man's Desiring.' There are any number of choices you can make. And then there are the solos to consider."

"I-I'll think about it." She was beginning to wonder if she would ever be able to think again.

"And the music for the reception?"

"Hire a string quartet. I'm sure you know of a good one."

"Yes, of course, but usually for a wedding of your type an orchestra is used."

"Okay."

Margaret leaned closer, obviously worried now. "I assume your gown is already being made?"

"No. I plan to make one or two calls and have something sent over." Margaret was staring at her. Apparently there was something the woman was expecting her to say or do. She just wished she knew what it was. "It will be fine. Really. Nothing to worry about. What else?"

"Well . . ." Margaret thumbed through her notebook.

She could feel Cale's steady gaze, and her nerves began to unravel, one by one. "Look, I'm going to leave all the details in your hands. Whatever you decide will be fine with me."

The older woman's mouth fell open. "You mean *all* the details?"

"With the exception of Kylie's dress."

"But—"

"No, really, that's how I want it. I trust you. I know you'll do a beautiful job."

Margaret closed her mouth and the notebook. "Very well, my dear. I'll get started immediately. But I insist that you approve all my choices."

"Fine."

"And we need to set up a photographic session immediately. Within the next day or two. And your dress must be ready for that."

"Sure. Okay."

"Uh, I don't suppose you care who the photographer is?"

"Not really. We usually use Anton Karban, but whoever you choose will be fine." She needed to go check on Kylie. But most of all she needed to get away from Cale's penetrating gaze.

Margaret glanced at her calendar, her expression stating that she obviously didn't understand, but would do her best anyway. "Very well. I'll make the appointment and get back to you. It should be as soon as possible, say in the next day or two. You'll have your wedding gown by then?"

"I'll have it tomorrow morning. You can make the appointment for the afternoon if you like."

Margaret gave a slight shake of her head. "I'll alert the photographer, but I'll wait until you get the gown to firm up the appointment." She turned to Cale. "It was very nice meeting you."

Cale came away from the table he had been leaning against. "You too. I'd appreciate you running the arrangements past me once they're set."

"Certainly, I'd be happy to."

Cale waited while Margaret took her leave from Jo and left, then turned to her. "You know it's funny, but it's been my experience that a bride-to-be loves planning her wedding."

He'd spoken thoughtfully, without sarcasm, but Jo's nerves were too raw to accept his statement with equanimity. "And how many wedding plans have you witnessed firsthand?"

"A couple," he said, his tone mild as hers had been harsh. "My two sisters—they each planned their respective weddings down to the last twig."

"Twig?"

"One was an autumn wedding. The point is—"

"The point is the time frame for my wedding is very short and I'm simply too busy to plan every detail. Don't read anything else into it. The moment Brett and I exchange vows is what's important. Nothing else."

The look he sent her made her feel like a butterfly pinned to a board.

"You're a very interesting woman, Jo. Mesmerizing, actually." Before she could think of a response, he strolled to her and dropped a kiss on her lips. "See you later." He passed his thumb over her bottom lip, rubbing away the moisture he had put there. "If you get lonely tonight and want to talk . . . or whatever . . . you know where I'll be."

"Whatever?" she asked, still reeling from the impact of the light, brief kiss.

"Whatever," he repeated, his meaning spelled out in the heated darkness of his eyes.

He left then, taking with him his unique electrical current that wrapped around her whenever he was near. She let out a long breath of relief. She'd never met a man who exuded more energy and was capable of creating more stress. And heat.

Somehow she had to get through the next couple of weeks without getting more involved with him than she already was. Somehow . . .

With a groan she reached for her address book and single-mindedly flipped through it until she found the number she was looking for. A minute later, she was talking to a buyer of a well-known department store with whom she had dealt many times over the years.

"I trust your judgment, Connie. Just send something nice. You know my size and style. I've given you the general guidelines. You shouldn't have any problems."

"But a wedding dress!" came the horrified and baffled response. "And you're a *designer*."

"Right on both counts."

"But it seems to me that you would want to design it yourself. Or at the very least pick it out."

Jo banked down her impatience. Why were people having such a hard time accepting that she didn't want to plan her wedding? "You're right. Normally I would want to, but I'm trying to take care of so many other details and the time is getting shorter and shorter. The bottom line is I need the dress as soon as possible for my photographs."

"Well, okay. I'll do my best."

"Thanks. I knew I could count on you. Oh and listen—send it by messenger. I need it this afternoon if possible. In the morning at the very latest. You have exquisite taste, Connie. Whatever you choose I'll be ecstatic about."

Outside the studio, Cale leaned against the wall by a window, listening, his expression grim.

He'd trusted his instincts all his life, and now those instincts were telling him that something wasn't right with the picture he was seeing.

At the same time, and for practically the *first* time ever in his life, he had to question his instincts.

He wasn't exactly objective when it came to Jo. Since the first moment he'd laid eyes on her he'd been involved with her. He'd had no choice. He'd looked at her and in an instant wanted her. Nothing had ever been so breathtakingly clear and simple to him. Or so urgent.

And because of this, he had to ask himself if there really was something wrong. Or did he just badly want to believe there was to justify his interest in her. He didn't know.

He had a deep and profound need to protect, and this need had been with him for as long as he could remember. As he'd grown older the need had only become stronger. It had led him to his profession.

It had led him to Jo. . . .

Would he really be able to watch her marry another man?

No.

But he would have to. He had no choice.

FOUR

Quietly Cale slipped into the sunroom by a side door. Jo, Abigail, and David were there, along with a policeman who had just finished questioning David.

According to Cale's man at the gate, the policeman was a Lt. Robinson and he was there to question the Damarons about a party held a couple of weeks ago at the home of one of their neighbors. It seemed that a young man who might or might not have attended had disappeared. It didn't sound too serious to Cale and strictly speaking the questioning was none of his business, but that hadn't stopped him from walking up to the house to see what was going on.

He made a quick assessment of the situation and decided everything looked routine. There were no tensions or undercurrents from

Jo, Abigail, or even David. In fact David had retreated to an easy chair by a window to read the morning paper, though Cale was positive the younger man was still monitoring the conversation. David missed very little, he judged.

It had taken him only a couple of inquiries to discover that David was Abigail's godson. Very much an extended family member, he came and went from her home without any schedule. But no one knew what if anything he did for a living. Not that it mattered, he supposed.

Cale relaxed back against the doorjamb and listened.

Abigail created several quick circles in the air with her cigarette holder. "Captain Robinson, exactly what—?"

"That's Lieutenant, ma'am."

The smile she bestowed upon him held a wealth of sympathy and encouragement. "That's really too bad, but you shouldn't worry. I'm sure you'll be a captain any day."

"Thank you. Now—"

"But you're a lieutenant? Isn't it unusual for someone as important as you to come out on something like this when there's no evidence of foul play? That is what you said, isn't it?"

Cale grinned to himself. That Abigail was one sharp cookie, no matter which way you sliced her.

"That's what I said, Mrs. Damaron. We found Glen Keenan's car parked on a back road near our airport, but nothing appears the least bit suspicious other than the fact that no one seems to know where he is. I'm here unofficially as a friend of the family."

"That's very nice of you," she said approvingly.

"Thank you. Now about the party at the Seaberg estate—"

"Oh." She glanced at her empty cigarette holder as if hoping to find a cigarette. "I wasn't there."

Robinson checked his notes. "But I thought you said it was a wonderful party."

The manner in which her eyes widened clearly indicated her astonishment that he even thought to question her on the matter. "Well, it *was*. Absolutely. *Everyone* said so, and of course I'm not surprised. It would be quite beyond the Seabergs to throw a bad party. I remember once many years ago—"

"Yes, I'm sure. Thank you, Mrs. Damaron. You've been a big help." He turned to Jo, who was sitting near her aunt. "But you *were* there —do I understand that correctly?"

"Yes, I was," she said, her tone pleasant. "For a brief time. I think I was there about an hour, just long enough to say hello to some friends."

She seemed aloof and untouchable, her

cool, elegant beauty a counterpoint to the warmth of the morning sunlight and the vivid colors of the flowers and cushions that abounded in the room. And even amidst the freshly brewed coffee and just-picked flowers it was her scent that reached him. But then hers was an impossible-to-ignore-or-to-forget fragrance that had somehow, someway, become imbedded in his senses. It was the first scent he smelled when he awoke in the morning, the last he smelled at night before falling asleep.

Last night his man on the gate had called to report that Brett Saunders had arrived, and it was an hour and a half later before he called back to tell him Saunders had left. Realistically he had had slim-to-none hope that she would really come to him, but fool that he was, he had still waited for her. And waited. . . .

Just then she looked at him. He could detect no surprise in the silvery green depths of her eyes at seeing him there. Nor was there the remoteness that had characterized her gaze when he had first met her. At least she was aware of him now, aware but not accepting.

Cale heard Robinson ask her, "Did you see Glen Keenan while you were there?"

"No."

"Are you sure?"

"Yes. There were a lot of people there that night, but even so . . ." Her words trailed off as she got up and strolled over to a vase filled with fresh flowers. Stem by stem she began to rearrange them.

"Even so?" the lieutenant prompted.

She glanced at him. "Even so I'm positive I didn't see him. If I had, I would have remembered. Why do you think he was there?"

"He used his credit card at a gas station located within five miles of the Seabergs'. The attendant reported that Glen mentioned the Seabergs' party."

She pulled a long-stemmed red rose from the arrangement. Several of its petals fluttered to the table. She tossed the rose into a nearby wastebasket. "I suppose he could have stopped by the party or he could have just as easily changed his mind and headed off in ten other directions."

"That's why I'm checking," Robinson said. "What about your sister, Miss Damaron?"

"She was at the party, too, and she might have seen Glen. They do know each other." She rubbed a petal from another rose between her thumb and forefinger. Cale wondered if she knew that her skin felt just as soft, just as velvety.

Abigail nodded her agreement with her niece. "Glen is one of the boys Kylie knows from school. He's always been a wild boy, in and out of trouble, but it's such a shame about his disappearance. A real shame. I know his parents are worried sick."

"Yes, ma'am. Miss Damaron, did you and your sister go to the party together?"

"No. We both went alone and at different times."

Abigail spoke up again. "And that's quite all right that they did that, you know. Our families have known each other forever and the kids grew up going in and out of each other's homes. Joanna and Kylie have lived here for almost thirteen years. Going into the Seaberg home is almost like going into their own."

Quite a feat, Cale thought, considering the homes were miles apart. But Abigail's friends and their children lived privileged lives and he was sure that when the kids had been younger they had had all sorts of ways of getting from one house to the next, starting with a fleet of bicycles, moving to their own horses, and going right up the scale to family chauffeurs. Later, of course, there would have been cars.

So what was a guy who had been raised in a nice middle-class neighborhood, doing, being attracted to Jo Damaron? He had no idea.

"And we didn't leave together either," Jo was saying, "but she did arrive home shortly after I did."

"How shortly?"

"I couldn't tell you. I rarely look at my watch on the weekends."

"Give me an estimate."

Her fingers closed around a rose bloom,

crushing it. Cale's brows drew together as his gaze sharpened. Was it his imagination or was Jo tense? Odd. Moments before she'd seemed so cool.

Releasing the rose so that its yellow petals joined the red ones on the table, she shrugged nonchalantly. "Could have been thirty minutes or so."

Lt. Robinson scanned his notes, then looked back at her. "Okay, that's all I need from you for now, but I'd like to see your sister."

"I'm sorry, that's not possible. As I told you, she isn't feeling well."

"I only need a few minutes of her time."

"I understand, but it won't be possible today."

"Tomorrow?"

"Perhaps." A stem broke in her hand. She pulled it quickly from the arrangement and threw it into the wastebasket. "I'll have her give you a call as soon as she can."

She *was* tense, Cale thought.

As if she sensed his scrutiny her gaze flicked to him, then back to the police lieutenant. "Is that all?"

"Except for the few questions I have for your sister."

Her smile for the lieutenant was lovely and gracious, but it also brooked no argument.

"I'm sure she'll be able to give you a call within the next few days."

Abigail had followed Jo's gaze to Cale and had given him a warm smile of greeting. But now she said, "David, would you please show Lieutenant Robinson out?"

"Sure."

Before David could rise from his chair, Cale straightened away from the door. "If you don't mind, David, I'd like to walk Lieutenant Robinson out."

"No problem." David folded his paper.

"And you are?" Robinson asked Cale, seeing him for the first time.

He handed him one of his cards. "I'm handling the security for Miss Damaron's wedding."

Abigail rose. "I'm due at Marjorie McConnel's for lunch."

"I'm on the way into town," David said, pushing himself out of the chair and sauntering over to her. "I'll drop you if you'd like."

"Thank you, David, but I think I'll drive. It's such a beautiful day I'd like to take the convertible and put the top down."

His lips quirked. "All right, but don't let that foot of yours get too heavy."

"We'll see," Abigail responded noncommittally.

David looked at Jo. "Can I drop you anywhere or do you need an errand run?"

She had no intention of going anywhere, not until she had discovered how Cale's conversation with the lieutenant had gone. She shook her head. "Thanks, anyway."

"Sure."

"By the way, Joanna," Abigail said, "I heard from Wyatt and Sinclair this morning. They're in the Far East at the moment, but they'll be here in time for the wedding, as will everyone else in the family. As for the invitations, we've gotten less than a handful of negative replies."

"That's good." For a moment she allowed herself the luxury of once again considering asking Jonah, Wyatt, Sin, and the rest of her cousins for help. But, no. She'd already considered the situation very carefully.

Her family moved through the world like panthers, big, powerful, and, when provoked, extremely dangerous. She had only to ask if she needed any type of help and it would instantly be hers. But in this case finesse was called for, and she was convinced she'd have a better chance at success if she proceeded alone.

She had a lot to accomplish before the wedding and the arrival of her family, and Kylie had to recover her balance and her mental strength.

In her peripheral vision she saw Abigail and David leave the room. But her focus was on Cale as he escorted Lt. Robinson out. A fine tremor shook her. She turned and headed

toward the sideboard for a cup of coffee. She
had drunk an entire cup by the time Cale returned to the room.

And she had known he would return, looking for her. How had she known? She had no
idea. Except as wrong and as impossible as she
knew it was, there was a connection between
the two of them, indefinable, but very, very
tangible.

He slipped his hands into his pockets and
regarded her thoughtfully. "If wishing and
wanting could have gotten you to come to me
last night, you would have."

Her fingers tightened on the delicate china
handle of the cup as she remembered her own
battle. She'd lain in bed and actually wondered
what it would be like to make love to him. She
turned away to set her coffee cup down on the
sideboard, then lightly rested her hand on its
edge.

"You must have known I wouldn't." She
added beneath her breath, "Couldn't."

"I mentioned wishing and wanting. I didn't
say I *expected* you to."

She cleared her throat. "What'd you talk to
the lieutenant about?"

"Just checking on a few things about that
kid who's missing."

"Why?"

"Curious. It's too bad about him, isn't it?"

"Yes."

"What's your guess? You think he cashed in part of his trust fund and flew down to Cabo with a few of his friends for his own little spring break?"

"I really don't know."

"You sound very casual about this whole thing. I suppose it isn't unusual for you people to lose guests."

Her hand jerked slightly, but it was enough to send the coffee cup tumbling from its saucer and off the sideboard to the floor. "You people?"

His gaze dropped thoughtfully to the cup lying on the floor, then went back to her. He'd made nothing more than a casual statement without any underlying meaning. Obviously his earlier feeling that she was tense was correct. Why? Because of him? "I was referring to those of you who live in this area and wondering if it was usual for your guests to be missing now and again."

"Hardly ever. And do you often paint large groups of people with the same brush?"

He smiled. "Hardly ever."

She stared at his smile. It was the kind that could melt a woman's heart one moment and break it the next. "I'm not at all casual about the fact that Glen is missing. His family has my entire sympathy. I can't imagine how they're getting through this. . . ." Her voice trailed off.

Something was bothering her, yet as far as he knew there was only one fly currently in her ointment and that was *him*. Practically on the eve of her wedding, a man had come into her life and couldn't seem to leave her alone. Given those circumstances he supposed any woman would be upset. Any woman, that is, except Jo. No. She struck him as being able to handle a man, *any* man, no matter how strongly he came on to her.

Under normal circumstances she would be able to.

Why did that phrase keep coming back to him? Clearly she wasn't operating under normal circumstances. She was about to be married. Still . . .

He slipped his hand into the pocket of his slacks. "Lieutenant Robinson is trying to reconstruct the night of the Seabergs' party. He's talking to as many people as he can from the party to see if, among other things, he can figure out who the last person was who saw Glen before he disappeared."

"Are you telling me because you don't think I figured that out?"

Actually he wasn't sure why he was telling her. "Just small talk, Jo. That's all."

"Police investigations aren't small talk." She stooped to pick up the cup. When she'd knocked it to the floor, it had chipped and the handle had broken off.

"No, they're not, but since you don't know anything about the case it shouldn't bother you." He paused. "But you are concerned about something, aren't you? What is it?"

As she straightened she gave a short laugh. "First I'm casual and now I'm concerned?"

"I don't know. It just seems to me that for a woman about to participate in one of the happiest events of her life you're very tense."

"I'm concerned about Glen, that's all." She saw him looking at her with a slightly perplexed expression. "I would be concerned about anyone who was missing, no matter how well I knew or didn't know them."

He kept hoping that if he stared at her long enough, talked to her long enough, then maybe, *maybe* he could figure her out. "Do you think your sister knows anything about Glen?"

Jo shook her head. "No."

"Have you asked her?"

"What is this? An interrogation? Are you trying to do Lieutenant Robinson's job for him?"

"Habit."

She sighed. "Kylie's friends have had Glen's disappearance on their grapevine for over a week. She's naturally concerned."

"Yet she wasn't even up to seeing Robinson for a few minutes?"

"Not today."

"She must be very ill," he said speculatively.

"She just needs rest right now, that's all. She's going to be fine."

"That's good to hear." He paused. "You've never shown me a picture of her." He nodded to the sideboard behind her. "Is that her?"

"Yes." She reached for the picture he had indicated and handed it to him.

The picture revealed a lovely young girl embraced by wind and sunlight, with a delicate silver streak running through her hair, stating to the world that she was a Damaron.

He looked back at Jo. "In a few years she's going to be truly beautiful, just like her sister."

"Excuse me. I have a lot of things to do today." She started from the room, but his next words stopped her.

"Brett didn't stay long last night, did he?"

She twirled around. "You timed him?"

"The guard at the gate noted his arrival and departure time."

"He's my fiancé," she snapped. "Not some workman you need to keep track of."

"No," he agreed, replacing the picture, then advancing toward her. "It's not strictly necessary, but I guess you could say I was very interested."

"There was no way I would have come to you, Cale."

He stopped in front of her. "Do you really

love him that much?" His voice was soft, almost caressing.

"I'm going to marry him, aren't I?"

"I'm not sure that's an answer to my question. Why don't you try again."

"I wouldn't marry a man I didn't love."

Slowly he lifted his hands to frame her face. "I thought I knew myself before I met you. I firmly believed that a woman who belongs to another man was out of bounds. Wife, girlfriend, fiancée, it didn't matter. I never even thought about encroaching. But then we met and I realized I didn't know myself as well as I thought." He shifted his stance, spreading his legs so that he was eye level with her. "I wish I could tell you that your upcoming marriage makes a difference to me, Jo, that it will make me back off. But the truth is it doesn't." He lifted his fingers and lightly touched her cheek. "I want you more with every minute that passes."

Something was wrong, Cale thought the next evening, keeping his gaze on the distant taillights of Jo's car as he drove through the night behind her. He might be crazy and he definitely felt like an idiot, but he couldn't shake the idea that something was wrong. When he'd seen her getting into her car a short time earlier and hurriedly driving away, he had decided to follow her.

Still, despite his instincts telling him differently he couldn't quite wrap his mind around the idea that Jo could be in trouble. Maybe it was because he couldn't imagine what kind of trouble she could be in that her money and family couldn't get her out of. Or maybe it was simply because he couldn't tolerate so much as a hint of an idea that she might be in trouble.

His protective instincts at work again, going full throttle.

At any rate, here he was unapologetically following a woman who didn't want anything to do with him, a woman about to marry a man named Brett Saunders, a man he had checked out.

Saunders, he had discovered, was a midlevel executive for Damaron International. He also rented a carriage house on one of the nearby estates, which put him in a perfect position to be a fixture on the area social circuit. He always seemed to have money and drove an expensive sports car. Certainly nothing odd about any of the information, not for someone marrying Jo.

Twenty times today he had made the decision to let one of his men take over the Damaron job and twenty times today he had reversed his decision. The truth was simple and incredibly stupid—he didn't want her to go out of his life until she had to.

The thought made his hands tighten on the steering wheel; he refocused his gaze on her car's taillights. For all he knew, she could be meeting Brett in town for dinner. Or she could be checking on some aspect of the wedding. There could be a hundred innocent explanations, but he didn't think so.

He saw her car take a turn, and he speeded up so that he wouldn't lose her. Minutes later, she wheeled into the parking lot of a diner that looked a mere step above a dive. By the time he found an unobtrusive spot to park, he'd lost sight of her.

On foot he maneuvered himself to a corner of the parking lot until he could see into the diner and more important see her, although he didn't have a clear line of vision to her. While keeping to the cover of shrubs, trees, and cars, he shifted his position several times, trying to get the best angle.

She was seated in a back corner of the diner at a booth with an older man. They weren't touching; instead they sat rather formally across from each other, as if they were conducting business. During the next thirty minutes the only breaks in that formality came during the times the pretty redheaded waitress would sashay by with a friendly smile and word for the man, plus a coffee warm-up. At one point he laughingly and lightly slapped the waitress on the rump. Cale hoped it was a sign the two of them knew each other; he'd find out.

Cale returned his focus to the man and decided that he looked like every cop he had ever known. In this particular case the man was old enough to be retired. Perhaps another useful thing to know.

He watched them for the next fifteen minutes as Jo talked with the man. He couldn't tell anything from her demeanor. At this distance she seemed as cool and composed as she ever did. But he had come to believe that her composure was nothing more than a carefully constructed facade. In many ways he hoped he was wrong. But there was also a twisted, perverse part of him that hoped he was right. At least she'd need him then.

He saw both Jo and the man stand up, and she reached to shake the man's hand. Cale returned to his car, slid down in his seat, and waited until she and the man drove away in their respective vehicles. Then he climbed out of his car and went into the diner.

It took only a short time and a generous tip for a single cup of coffee before he got the information he was after. The man Jo had met with was one Alvin Shaw, a retired cop and currently owner of his own private investigation firm.

FIVE

"Good morning, Cale." Abigail directed a welcoming smile at him as he climbed the flagstone steps to the back terrace. "Please join me."

"Thank you." He dropped into a cushioned chair across the width of the glass table from her and sat back while Marian, one of the Damarons' maids, produced his breakfast—a cup of steaming coffee and a plate of fruit and sweet rolls. He had ordered it when Abigail had called him at seven this morning and requested his presence.

It was a crystalline spring morning, the air soft and mild and carrying fragrant scents from the many gardens that abounded on the estate. Abigail, Cale noted, was her usual vision in red from her hair to fingernails to her flowing caftan. He didn't imagine too many people refused an invitation from her, even if they didn't work for her.

"How have you been doing, Cale? We don't get to see enough of you. You must come to dinner one night. In fact often. It's not good that you're alone so much."

Great, he thought. His idea of a nightmare would be sitting at a table with Jo, surrounded by other people, possibly even her fiancé. His idea of a dream, on the other hand, would be to have her all to himself for a full night. He avoided answering her by dropping a thick file folder on the table and pushing it across to her. "You asked for an update on the security. It's all outlined in there."

Nodding absently she opened the file and idly flipped through the pages. Now and again she would stop to scan, holding the page as far away from her as possible and squinting her eyes to read.

"May I help you read anything?"

"No, no. I can see quite well, thank you. This looks very comprehensive. Are you having any problems?"

"None at all."

"You're coordinating the RSVP's and gifts with my assistant?"

"Yes, or Jo."

"And you've also met Jo's wedding coordinator and she's giving you all the information you're asking for?"

"Yes."

"I'm very impressed with your operation. All of your men have been, without fail, very polite and helpful."

"That's good to hear."

She closed the file and fixed him with a twinkling smile. "I called your uncle the day you came for your interview."

He grinned. He had known it wouldn't take her long to get to the real reason she had wanted to see him. "Yes, I know. Raymond told me."

"How extremely vexing of him. He wouldn't tell me a thing." She gestured in disgust. "I couldn't believe it. I've always been able to get anything out of him, but on the subject of your personal life he was an absolute sphinx." She chewed thoughtfully on her bottom lip. "Which of course leads me to believe there is something about you worthy of hiding."

Cale broke out laughing. "What interesting thought processes you have."

"Well, I ask you—why else would he refuse to discuss you?"

"Maybe because there's nothing of any real interest to discuss."

She pointed a ringed finger at him. "I don't believe it for a minute. A man like you would have an amazing personal history—wives, lovers, fiancées, others."

"Others?" With a chuckle he shook his head. "I'm sorry if the truth is not as riveting as you'd hoped."

She gestured dismissively. "The point is I got nowhere with Raymond." She paused for a moment, her displeasure and puzzlement over the fact apparent in her expression. "At any rate he suggested that I ask you what I want to know."

Cale spread his hands out. "So ask. I'm an open book."

She gave a snort which somehow managed to remain within the bounds of what could be termed ladylike. "Open book, my eye. Sell it to someone who's not an old horse trader from way back."

His grin widened. "Horse trader? You, Abigail?"

"I've traded horses, men, jewels, lies, truths." She shrugged. "The concept is pretty much the same."

He laughed. "Why am I not surprised?"

Suddenly Abigail lifted her hand and waved. "There's Joanna and Brett. I didn't know he was coming this morning."

He turned his head and saw the couple acknowledging Abigail's wave with their own. They were strolling across the lawn, Brett's arm around Jo, her body tucked familiarly against his. A surge of uncontrollable jealousy coiled in his gut.

"They make a nice-looking couple, don't they?" Abigail said thoughtfully.

He didn't answer. He couldn't. He felt caught in an inescapable trap of desire and frustration—wanting her, yet knowing he wasn't going to be able to have her.

None of it seemed right. Not his desire for her, not her fiery reaction to him, and definitely not the fast approaching wedding.

Everything was out of kilter. The world was spinning the wrong way and somehow he had to regain his balance, his focus, his peace of mind. That or give in and go with the craziness.

Abigail settled back into her chair. "I'm sure they'll come join us in a few minutes. In the meantime let's get back to you."

Preoccupied with trying to get the knots in his stomach to untie, he sipped at his coffee. Its warmth didn't help at all. "Not my favorite subject, but okay."

"You don't want to talk about yourself?" She popped a grape in her mouth. "Then what about Joanna as a subject? Would that be better?"

Infinitely better, he thought, giving her his full attention again. "Sure. What would you like to tell me?"

"You misunderstand. I want you to tell me."

"Tell you what?"

"I want you to tell me why you have such a strange effect on Joanna."

Once more he glanced toward the happy couple. They had stopped and were facing each other. Brett was holding Jo's hand, and he had a smile on his face as he listened to whatever it was she was saying to him. Turning away from the sight, he took another gulp of coffee. "Could you be more specific with that, Abigail?"

"Joanna hasn't been acting like herself lately, and it started about the time you showed up."

"Your niece is a very lovely woman, Abigail. And a very *engaged* woman. If you believe something is wrong, why don't you ask Jo what it is?"

"I have, and she's told me that nothing is wrong."

"But you don't believe her?"

"No."

He glanced again at Jo and Brett. Her hand was extended, and she appeared to be caressing his face. The jealousy coiled tighter, so much so, he had to resist rubbing his stomach to relieve the distress. There was no rhyme or reason to any of this, no answer as to why she had the ability to compel him so, only that she drew him as no other woman ever had. "Maybe it's just prewedding jitters."

"You have to understand, Cale. I've seen

her incredibly sad and almost inconsolable
when her parents and aunts and uncles were
killed. I've seen her happy. But I've never seen
her rattled."

The news that Abigail was picking up on
the same vibes as he darkened his mood. Not
that he had needed the corroboration. He covered his troubled state of mind with a calm
tone. "But then you've never seen her about to
be married, have you?"

"No, I haven't—"

"Well, there you go." He was giving her
the alternative he had tried more than once to
give himself. It hadn't worked for him, but it
might work for Abigail.

She picked up her cigarette holder and contemplated its end as if hoping at any moment a
cigarette would appear.

He didn't believe what he had said, Cale
reflected, and neither did she. Unfortunately
she didn't seem to know any more than he did.
In fact he probably knew more. For instance he
knew Jo had met with a private investigator last
night, who, he had learned, had a low profile
but a good reputation.

"Good morning, Aunt Abigail."

"Kylie!" Abigail turned and held her hand
out to the slight, pale young woman who had
just walked out on the terrace from the house.
"How *wonderful* to see you up and out. You
must be feeling better."

"Yes, I am." Kylie bent and kissed her aunt's cheek then straightened and waved at her sister in the distance.

"Jo didn't mention that you were going to come downstairs today."

"No, I thought I'd surprise her."

"She's going to be delighted. She's had her hands full lately."

"I know." Kylie extended her hand to Cale. "Hello, I'm Kylie Damaron. And you're Cale Whitfield, the person in charge of the security for Jo's wedding. Nice to meet you."

"Nice to meet you too." She was charming and had impeccable manners, and it took only one look for him to know that the reports of her illness hadn't been exaggerated. Her features were drawn, and there were dark circles beneath her blue eyes. His sympathy was immediately aroused. And also his curiosity. Beneath the charm and manners she was on guard. Why? he wondered. Was it because he was a stranger?

"I'm glad to hear that you're feeling better," he said.

"Thank you."

She was past slim, he observed as she sank into a chair not too far from him, with baby-blond hair as fine as an angel's and skin an ivory so translucent, he could see the tiny blue veins beneath the skin of her temple. But even recovering from an illness she was undeniably lovely.

The attentive Marian appeared beside Kylie with a glass of juice and toast for her. "Thank you, Marian." She tossed her hair behind her shoulder and narrowed her eyes against the daylight. "Here come Jo and Brett."

Cale didn't trust himself to turn and watch them climbing the stairs to the terrace. Before he witnessed close-up her interacting with Brett, he badly needed to get himself under control.

"Good morning, everyone," he heard Brett say, his tone jovial.

He didn't look at Saunders, but when it came to Jo he couldn't resist sneaking a glance at her. She was wearing a short green sheath, very simple and elegant with only a minimum of gold jewelry. But then, with that rock sparkling on her finger she didn't need anything else.

She went straight to Kylie and gave her a long hug. "I'm so *glad* to see you out here." As she drew back, a few strands of her pale hair caught and mingled in Kylie's, their silver and blond tones blending exquisitely. "How are you feeling, honey?"

"Just a little shaky but otherwise fine."

When Jo straightened away, Brett bent to

give Kylie a hug of his own. "Your sister's been very worried about you."

A faint, wry smile touched Kylie's lips. "I know, but I wanted to wait until most of the work had been done on the wedding before I came out of my room."

Brett laughed with appreciation. "Clever girl."

Jo chose a chair next to her sister. "Have you eaten yet?"

Kylie indicated the plate in front of her. "I'm starting on toast."

"But you need something more nourishing. How about a cheese omelet? Shall I ask the cook to make you one?"

"Let me see how I do with the toast first."

Brett reached over the table to shake Cale's hand. "Good to see you again. How are things going? Any problems?"

"Not a one." Hostility crawled along his skin at the man's presence. That Saunders was a bit too smooth in his estimation wasn't exactly grounds for indictment. Yet he disliked him more each time he saw him. But as he'd admitted to himself before, he honestly would never like him, no matter what. He was going to marry Jo and for that very fact alone he could easily hate him.

Jo—he glanced at her to find her watching him. "How are you, Jo?"

"Very well, thank you. I didn't expect to see you this morning."

Prickly, he thought. Very prickly. He smiled. "Abigail invited me."

"I see."

The lady was displeased, he thought, gratified. She *did* feel something for him. She couldn't ignore him; good or bad, she reacted to him. And either way, she wasn't indifferent to him.

"Where's David?" Brett asked, taking his own seat.

"He's gone away for a few days." Abigail's fork hovered over a slice of melon before stabbing it.

Brett's laugh held a slight edge. "David doesn't seem to follow any pattern in anything he does. Lucky man who doesn't have to work."

Jo was still looking at Cale and didn't comment, but Abigail said, "David has things to do, but he'll be back in time for the wedding."

"Excellent."

Abigail glanced at Kylie. "Did he look in on you before he left?"

She nodded. "He woke me to say good-bye."

Brett's remarks told Cale that Brett wasn't completely on the inside yet. However, once Brett wed into the family it would be a different story.

He was the outsider. And Jo's wedding would come and go and he would move on to other jobs and the Damarons would remain the close-knit clan they had always been. And he still wouldn't know them any better than he knew them now.

Not that it mattered. There was only one of them he really wanted to know better.

And he had so many questions: Why had she kissed him and then gone on kissing him? Why was she seeing a private investigator? Why were there times she seemed tense enough to snap in two? And why in hell was she marrying Saunders?

Damn it all, he *cared* about the answers. And because he did he had become aware that he was setting himself up for heartbreak.

The idea amazed him. He was a cautious man by nature. Only when he perceived danger did his instincts kick in and he behave in a manner others might perceive as reckless. But with Jo he was acting neither cautious nor protective. And even more amazing, he was beginning to think it just might be too late to think about protecting himself.

The portable phone lying by Abigail's hand rang, bringing him out of his reverie.

She answered it. "Jonah, darling, how are you?" She listened for a moment, then threw back her head and laughed. "Yes, I'm behaving myself and as a result I'm a complete bore. As a matter of fact I'm even boring myself. But stand by, because the first opportunity I get I'm going to break loose and do some serious damage." She listened, then laughed again. "Where are you?" She looked at Jo, silently including her in the conversation. "Oh, you've moved on to Hong Kong? I expect you know that Wyatt and Sinclair are somewhere in the area." She nodded at something he said. "And when can we expect you?" She listened. "Wonderful. That will be perfect. Jo? She's right here—I'll let you speak with her. See you soon. 'Bye for now." She extended the phone to Jo. "Your cousin wants to say hello. Oh, and tell him to be careful."

Jo took the phone as Brett quickly said, "Give Jonah my best."

"Hello, Jonah."

"Kylie," Cale said while Jo was occupied with the phone call. "Have you called Lieutenant Robinson yet?" To his surprise her ivory skin went chalk white.

He heard Jo say, "Just a minute, Jonah." She put her hand over the receiver and looked at him, her green eyes snapping with anger. "This is the first morning Kylie's been up, Cale. Give her a break."

He supposed it was natural that she was protective of her sister, Cale mused, especially since Kylie had been ill. But that didn't explain Kylie's loss of color. "I'm sorry. I didn't realize calling Lieutenant Robinson would be considered such an ordeal."

"Doing anything is if you've been sick." She removed her hand from the receiver. "I'm sorry, Jonah. What were you saying?"

Even though she had gone back to her conversation, her gaze remained on him. Curious about her attitude, he decided to push the matter a little further. "Kylie? Do you think you're going to feel up to calling Lieutenant Robinson soon? Because—"

"*Cale.*"

Ignoring Jo he went on. "If not, I can ask you a few questions and relay your answers to him."

"Leave her alone, Cale."

Brett covered Jo's free hand with his and patted it reassuringly. "It's all right. He's only trying to help the family. It's his job."

Abigail nodded. "He won't do a thing until Kylie's up to it, will you, Cale?"

"Of course not." Kylie looked like a deer caught in headlights, he noted. He leaned toward her. "I'm really sorry. I didn't mean to upset you."

"No . . . You didn't. I-I know I need to call him."

"Jonah, I've got to go for now." Her gaze skewered Cale as she listened to her cousin. "Great. See you in a few days."

"Give him my regards," Brett said sharply.

Almost simultaneously Abigail spoke up. "Don't forget to tell him what I said."

"Oh, Brett sends his regards, and Abigail says to be careful." She laughed. "I'll tell her. 'Bye." She punched the phone's off button and even though her gaze immediately went to Kylie, she spoke to Abigail. "Jonah said to tell you he's always careful."

"Ha! That boy doesn't know the meaning of careful. None of your cousins do."

"Did he say anything about me?" Brett asked. "You know, return my regards?"

"No, but then he was in a hurry. Kylie, why don't we go for a walk?"

"Excellent idea." Brett nodded approvingly. "Get some strength back into those limbs of yours, young lady."

"Stay with Brett, Jo," Kylie said, pushing back from the table. "I'd like to take a walk by myself."

"But—"

Brett squeezed Jo's hand, and his tone was tenderly teasing. "Give her some room to breathe, darling. She's going to be fine."

Jo visibly struggled with her emotions, and Cale understood. She wanted to help her sister and was extremely frustrated because she couldn't. It was similar to what he was feeling about her. Brett, however, didn't seem to notice what was going on with his fiancée. After a little pat on her hand he went back to his breakfast.

"I won't be long," Kylie said. "Then I'll probably go up to my room for a while."

"Do only what you feel up to doing, okay? I'll come find you when I can." Jo picked up a fruit knife and began absently tapping it against her plate.

"Okay. See everyone later." A chorus of good-byes accompanied the young girl as she descended the terrace stairs to the manicured lawn.

"Cale," Jo said, as soon as Kylie was out of earshot. "I will not tolerate you harassing my sister."

"Joanna," Abigail said with surprise, "what on earth are you talking about?"

Brett paused in the act of lifting a glass of juice to his lips. "Don't you think you're over-reacting?"

Cale didn't answer her immediately. Instead he sipped at his coffee, all the while watching her closely. She was like a lioness protecting her young, and if he understood anything at all it was the need to protect those more vulnerable than oneself. But what was she protecting Kylie from? After a moment he returned the cup to the table. "You interpreted my question to Kylie as harassing her? That's very interesting."

"And what would you call what you did?"

"I simply asked her a question with no harm intended. I'm sorry if you took it differently."

"Please excuse her, Cale." Abigail's expression was puzzled as she looked at her niece. "She's been very worried about her sister."

"Yes, I can see that she has." It was impossible for him to drop his gaze from Jo. The lights of anger blazing in her eyes made her arrestingly and intensely beautiful. She looked as if any moment she would come across the table at him, knife flashing. If they had been alone, he didn't doubt that she would have done just that. Pity that they weren't, he thought. Her unmasked anger might reveal more about her than her passion had so far.

"There's no need to apologize for me, Aunt Abigail."

"But she's right, Jo," Brett said. "The thing you need to focus on now is that Kylie is much better. In no time at all she's going to be one hundred percent."

"Listen to him," Abigail said. "For the first time in days Kylie came down to breakfast and is now taking a walk on her own. That's a huge improvement. She's soon going to be back to her old self, and isn't that exactly what the doctor told you? All she needed was to rest."

"Darling?" Brett reached out and turned Jo's face so that she was looking at him instead of Cale. "You've got nothing to worry about. Understand? *Nothing.*"

A barely noticeable tremor shook her, but Cale was concentrating so hard on her, there was no way he could have missed it, even as slight as it had been.

She exhaled slowly. "Of course. I'm sorry, Cale. I didn't mean to come down on you so hard."

"Oh, it wasn't all that hard," he said softly. "I felt no pain at all."

Brett's head snapped around to him, his expression alert. But when he spoke, his tone was even and pleasant. "With our wedding so close, I'm afraid all our nerves are showing."

Cale nodded politely. "Of course. That's understandable."

"Then everything's all settled," Abigail said, rising. "Joanna, is your wedding photo session this afternoon?"

"Yes."

"You didn't tell me that," Brett said, clearly delighted. "What location did you finally decide on?"

"I'm not sure. I told the photographer it was up to him."

"You're not supposed to know anyway," Abigail warned him teasingly. "If you know, you'll want to come and you're not supposed to see Joanna in her wedding dress until the wedding."

Brett laughed good-naturedly. "That's it then. I certainly don't want to be responsible for any bad luck at the start of our marriage."

Abigail nodded approvingly. "That's very wise. Now, I'm off to have my hair done."

"And I'm off to work," Brett said, following suit by also rising. "Jo, call me if you have any questions or problems."

"I will."

He bent and pressed a lingering kiss on her lips. When he was through, he lifted his head and whispered, "Promise?"

"I promise."

Jo smiled up at Brett, but Cale noted the strain around her mouth. She *had* overreacted to his talking to Kylie. He wished he knew why. He also wished he knew what had caused the strain he saw in her.

"Talk to you tonight." Lightly Brett trailed his hand over her hair in good-bye. "Whitfield," he said with a brisk nod, then strode into the house.

Jo clasped her hands in front of her on the table, then in a sudden movement pushed away from the table and surged to her feet. "I'm going to find Kylie."

"Wait a minute, Jo—"

Abigail interrupted him. "Joanna, just so you'll know, I won't be home until later this afternoon. Cale, remember you have an open invitation to dinner."

"Thanks, I'll remember." He turned around in his chair, following the older woman's stately progress as she made her way across the terrace toward the house. "Would you like me to have one of my men drive you to your appointment?"

"No, I would not. I'll be fine on my own."

"All right, but you've got your car phone. Don't hesitate to use it if you need anything at all."

About to disappear through a door she paused to laugh. "Now who's worrying too much?"

His teeth flashed as he grinned. "What can I say? It's my job." With a wave good-bye to her he straightened around. "Jo—"

He was alone at the table. Jo had vanished. Letting out a muttered curse, he scanned the area and spotted her already halfway across the lawn.

He caught up with her as she was about to disappear through an iron gate set amidst a high hedge. He reached for her and brought her to an abrupt stop. "Dammit, I asked you to wait."

She jerked free of him and rubbed her arm where his hand had been. He hadn't hurt her, but she felt as if somehow his touch had marked her. She tried to tell herself that her

breathlessness came from the run across the
lawn rather than the man in front of her. But
he was standing too close, heat and anger ra-
diating off his body with an assaulting power.
"Exactly what have I ever done or said to give
you the impression that I care what you say?"

"*Whoa.*" His brows shot up. "What's
wrong?"

There was nothing but gentleness in his
voice, nothing but thoughtfulness in his gaze,
but she wasn't soothed. How could anyone relax when they were, in essence, standing in the
middle of a minefield? "Nothing. It's just in
my experience, reason doesn't seem to get
through to you."

"If that's truly what you think then I
haven't made myself clear enough. *Everything*
you do or say gets through to me. I hear you, I
see you, I feel you . . ." He trailed off, caught
for a moment in the depths of her silvery green
eyes. Shadows lurked there. And . . . fear?
"What or who were you running from just
then, Jo?"

"I wasn't running from anything or anyone.
I was running *to*. Kylie."

"But I asked you to wait, just for a minute."

She'd heard him, but having him and Brett
at the same table had taken a heavy toll on her
nerves, and her ability to cope had been tem-
porarily shredded. The combination of people
at the table had been her worst nightmare.

Brett was predictable. Cale wasn't. Kylie needed special attention right now and had to be protected. Abigail was too observant. Everything could have blown up right then and there. "And are you so used to a woman doing what you say that you can't accept it when one doesn't?"

"When that woman's you, then, no, I can't."

Amazing, the two of them, she reflected sadly. It seemed beyond his ability to leave her alone. And it seemed beyond her ability to make him. Anyone else, she would snap her fingers and they'd be gone. But she and Cale were like pieces of flint, striking sparks and making fire. It wasn't something that could be dismissed or ignored.

She shook her head, silently chastising herself. She should have better control over the entire situation. "I'm sorry, but I've got a lot on my mind at the moment."

He shifted his stance, drawing closer to her. "And getting away from me will help you better deal with what's on your mind?"

She reached behind her for the gate. "Exactly."

"Why is that?"

Casually he stroked a strand of her hair away from her face, stopping her retreat simply by his touch. A sliver of heat shivered through her, followed by a cold surge of fear. What was she going to do about him? He'd offered to quit, and she'd said no. She couldn't ignore him. He wouldn't let her avoid him. He pushed buttons on her she hadn't known existed. He distracted her when she couldn't afford to be. Kylie and Brett should be her first and only priorities, yet she found herself thinking of him all the time . . .

"Why, Jo?"

The question jarred her, bringing her back to the moment. "Because . . . the things that are on my mind have nothing to do with you."

"Then let's don't talk. Let's make love."

The ground beneath her feet tilted, and her pulse accelerated. He'd finally given voice to what had lain unspoken between them from the moment they'd met. If only she didn't want to say yes so badly. "Don't," she whispered. "Don't ask."

"What if I beg?"

"This line of conversation leads nowhere." She swallowed against the sudden thickness in her voice. "Do you have any questions regarding the wedding?"

"As a matter of fact, I do. The question is *why?*"

She slid through the garden gate and was trying to shut it when he entered immediately behind her and closed it himself.

His lips slowly curved into a sensuous smile as he looked at her. "Don't want to hear me beg? Still trying to get away from me? Why, Jo?"

She stared at his mouth, remembering another garden they had been in and how his lips had felt on hers that night. They'd been firm and knowledgeable and hot, Lord, way too hot.

She started when he lifted his hand toward her. "Don't," he said softly. "I'm not going to hurt you."

There was a painful lump in her throat she couldn't make go away. "There are all different ways of hurting someone, Cale."

"And I'm not going to do any of them to you."

"You don't know. . . ."

"Then tell me."

A breath shuddered in and out of her. "No, you're right. You're not going to hurt me—I'm not going to let you—so there's nothing to tell."

"You're wrong," he murmured. "There's quite a bit to tell." He trailed his fingers down the side of her cheek, then unexpectedly dropped his hand to the top swell of her breast and flattened his palm against her heart. "Tell me it's not me that's making your heart beat so hard. Tell me and make me believe you."

Her heart thudded against his hand, and heat streamed through her body. How could she convince him when she couldn't convince herself? Still, she had to try. She stepped away so that his hand fell to his side. "It's not you," she said clearly and forcefully.

"I said make me believe you."

She'd been through worse challenges than Cale Whitfield. He wasn't going to change her mind about anything. He wasn't going to insinuate himself into her life. Most of all he wasn't going to make love to her. The trouble was, she wasn't fighting just him. She was also fighting herself. "I believe it—it doesn't matter if you don't."

"I wish I could agree."

He pulled her back to him, only this time he brought her against him and closed his hand over her breast, caressing her fullness with extraordinary expertise. Her nipple stiffened against his palm, and her breast began to ache.

"Jo?" A hint of pleading twisted through the gruffness of his voice. "Dammit, why won't you admit that you want me?"

The pleading surprised her, touched her, so much so, she had to harden her heart against it. "Because I don't."

"Is it that you don't? Or is it that you won't let yourself admit that you do?"

No. Only one word but she couldn't say it. He was forbidden to her, and the forbidden was always tantalizing. She couldn't want him, wouldn't. There was no place for him in her life now, and there especially was no place for him in her heart.

With a groan, he grasped her hips and pulled her against him. The long, hard ridge of his desire pressed into the lower part of her belly, and excitement slammed through her entire body.

His sure hands began to roam over her, memorizing the curving lines of her body, carrying and extending the heat to every part of her, the heat treacherous in its strength, addictive in its power. She gasped. "I can't take this."

"If I can, you can." The brown of his eyes turned nearly black. "It's my time for the truth, Jo. Right or wrong, my body hasn't known a moment of rest since I met you. Why should you go scot-free?"

She shook her head. "I'm *engaged* for God's sake. You're here for only one reason—my *wedding*! I don't come with the job."

"Tell me something I don't know. Talk to me," he said huskily. "And make it the truth."

"I *have* talked to you. I've talked to you until I don't know what to say anymore." She wanted to cry. Even as she was protesting, need for him throbbed in her. He could take away her pain if she let him, she thought, and it would be so simple. The garden was secluded. No one would interrupt them. They could make love among the flowers and for a while she would know bliss and ultimately release.

"Dammit, Jo, I know you feel what I feel."

"I'm sorry, but I don't."

Uttering a mild oath, he seized her by her upper arms, his grip hard, his eyes glittering. "Congratulations, Jo. If I wasn't crazy before, I'm certifiable now. *You* made me that way, and I can't think of one other person in my entire life who's ever come even close to doing that."

Trembling, dizzy, she couldn't think of a thing to say. She stared back at him, mesmerized by the fire and anger in his eyes. She'd never met anyone like him. He was an incredibly passionate man, and what he was making her feel for him was even stronger.

"I've tried to stay away from you," he said, his words forced from between his gritted teeth. "I've worn out the porch of the guest house, pacing at night, trying to keep myself from going to you. And I've tried like hell not to think you're in some kind of trouble, but I can't even come within a country mile of convincing myself."

One word stood out above the others. "*Trouble?* You think I'm in trouble?"

"Why else would you visit a private investigator? What is he doing for you, Jo? What's he looking for? Information? A person? Who?"

She hissed in a breath. "You followed me? You *followed* me?"

"Last night you met Alvin Shaw at a diner. I want to know why?"

"Cale . . ." Stunned and appalled, at a loss

for words, she broke away from him. It had been imperative that no one know she had hired Shaw. She'd gone to great lengths to keep the matter secret. And now . . .

No, she hastily reassured herself. Shaw wouldn't divulge anything to Cale. A private investigator didn't keep clients by sharing their secrets with others, even if the person doing the questioning was an ex-secret service agent. Plus if Cale had thought he could get anything out of Shaw, he wouldn't be questioning her now. By rights she shouldn't be that worried, except the situation was so delicately balanced that even what little he did know could prove disastrous. And the mere thought of the disaster that could follow frightened her to death.

There were dozens of reasons she could give him, but she was coming to realize that there was no reason he would accept. "It doesn't matter what reason I give you, the fact that I've asked you to leave me alone should be sufficient." Terrified of the consequences if she couldn't convince him, she fought back tears. If he continued on his present course, he would ruin several lives. "You need to concentrate on the job you're here to do for my wedding and get me out of your mind."

He stared at her for several moments. "Can you get me out of your mind?"

She tried to think of a lie he'd buy, a lie she

could actually force herself to say. But she couldn't. "No," she said. "I can't."

He pulled her to him and crushed his mouth down on hers and desire crashed through her, like waves in a storm, and her mind had to scramble to catch up with what her body was feeling. His tongue flicked out, then thrust deep into her mouth. Her knees weakened, her body softened, becoming so pliant, it seemed she would actually seep into him.

She was in trouble all right, and he was a big part of that trouble. He had come into her life at a time when it wasn't possible for him to be there, yet she couldn't bring herself to send him away. He touched her, affected her, turned her inside out with wanting, as no man ever had. Soon he would be gone. But until that time came . . .

Suddenly she gave in and admitted the full truth to herself. To meld with Cale and to be able to know the full extent of the pleasure he could give her and that she could give him was all that she wanted at this moment. On many indefinable but very basic levels she needed him, wanted him, *had* to have him.

Her breasts swelled and tightened as he kissed and touched her. An uncomfortable heaviness, almost a pain, filled her loins. The sun and breeze were warm on her skin, and inside, fire was raging out of control.

The back zipper of her dress slid down, then she felt his hand on her skin, caressing, molding, and his fingertips exploring the valley of her spine, bringing nerves to life beneath the skin, creating sensitivity and need.

She could no longer ignore what she was feeling, no longer deny herself. At that moment she wanted to give up everything and have him, except . . . there was one thing she couldn't give up, because there was much more at stake than just herself. She pulled her head back and drew in a ragged breath. "Cale."

He stilled, then slowly drew back his head until he could see her. "What?"

"I've got to ask you something. Now. It's about Shaw."

He shook his head, trying to clear it. "What about him?"

"Please, you must forget about him."

His brow wrinkled as he tried to absorb her words. "What?"

Her heart was pounding so hard, she could barely hear herself. "Forget you ever saw me with Shaw and give up efforts to investigate me or my family. It's important to me."

Her words were finally reaching him. He took her face between a thumb and forefinger and looked deep into her eyes. "What are you afraid of, Jo?"

She swallowed hard. She should have known. He was too smart not to question her proposition, even on the verge of lovemaking. "It's not what *I'm* afraid of. It's what I want. And I *want* you."

He hissed in a rough breath. "Do you mean that?"

"Yes. Yes, I do. I want to be with you, Cale, but—"

He brought his other hand up so that he framed her face. "And God knows I want to be with you. You know that. So what does any of that have to do with me forgetting Shaw?"

"Nothing. Everything. Shaw's doing me a personal favor, nothing for you to be concerned about. So do it for me, that's all I'm asking."

"That's all?"

"Yes."

Desire was surging through his body, clashing with his need to do whatever it took to ensure that she was happy and safe. And he would follow through on that—it didn't matter what she said or he said or what happened next. "Is this an either-or situation? Either I lay off Shaw or we won't make love?"

"*Jo!*"

She jerked around. "Kylie."

Kylie's eyes were huge with shock as she stared at the two of them. "My God, what are you doing?"

Her hands, she realized, were resting on Cale's shoulders. She abruptly pushed away from him and moved until she was separated from him by several feet. Kylie's appearance had startled her, but her blood was still running hot from wanting him. She'd been about to make love to him, and now she needed to clear her mind of him. To do that she needed to breathe without inhaling him. "Honey, I was looking for you, but then I ran into Cale." She glanced at him. "Cale, would you excuse us, please."

He looked from one to the other, then strolled over to her and pulled up her zipper. "All right."

Briefly she closed her eyes. She'd forgotten about the zipper.

"See you later."

When he was out of earshot, Kylie blurted out. "I don't understand, Jo. I thought you loved Brett. My Lord, you're about to marry him."

Her mind went into overdrive, searching for an explanation Kylie might accept. But she knew there was no explanation that would sound reasonable. "I don't know, honey. Maybe it's because I'm about to be married that something almost happened. But what you just saw—it means nothing. Just a little prewedding nerves, that's all."

"But if Brett ever found out—"

"He won't. I promise. What just happened —it's got nothing to do with him." True enough, but then with whom or what exactly did it have to do? "I guess we could file it under the category of one final harmless fling."

"If you say so." Kylie's expression was clearly dubious. "It's just so unlike you. You don't have flings."

She forced a light laugh. "So then what better time for me to have one than right before I'm about to be married?"

"I would think *any*time but then would be better."

She clasped her hands together. "What can I say? You're right."

Kylie chewed at a ragged fingernail. "You're still going to marry Brett?"

"Of course." Jo gently removed Kylie's finger from her mouth.

"You'll be careful with Cale, won't you? I mean, he doesn't seem the sort of man you should toy with."

"I know. You're right." She smiled. "And after all is said and done, nothing will probably happen between us anyway." She wished she could believe herself, but in reality she was dispensing reassurance when she felt none. "So—do you want to see the sketches I did for your dress? It's already being made, but you can see what it's going to look like from the sketch."

Kylie shook her head. "I'm going up to lie down for a while."

"Did you overdo it?"

"Maybe a little, but I'll be back down for dinner."

Jo heaved a sigh of relief. "Good girl. I'm very proud of you."

Kylie shook her head. "Don't be. I came down because of you, Jo. If I did what I really want to, I'd barricade my door and refuse to ever come out. But I can't. You're carrying so much on you. It's only fair that I try to help."

"I'm really, really glad."

Kylie's gaze was troubled. "Besides, I can't continue being such a coward, and I can't hide from the world forever. For one thing Lieutenant Robinson is not going to let me."

"Forget about him. You don't have to call him until you're ready. I can keep him at bay a little longer."

A wisp of hair blew across Kylie's face. She brushed it aside and grinned. "Being a big sister, huh?"

She slipped her arm around her and hugged her. "I took the job when you were born and as far as I can see it's a lifetime commitment."

SIX

"Turn your head this way, Joanna."

Jo did her best to oblige Anton Karban, one of the premier society photographers on the East Coast. Her parents had used him for every important event, as did Abigail. In fact she couldn't remember not knowing him. But still she couldn't help wishing she was somewhere, anywhere, else.

The afternoon sun hurt her eyes while its light made the pearls, iridescent sequins, and bugle beads on the pure white silk of her wedding gown glisten and gleam. Assistants darted to and fro between shots, setting her teeth on edge as they tweaked the cathedral train into order and fussed with the cloud of tulle that fell from the crown of her head and billowed out behind her for yards.

They adjusted and readjusted the pots and

trellises of cream hyacinths, pastel narcissi, pink-flushed roses, and raspberry-colored tulips that served as her background, an unnecessary gilding to Abigail's already glorious garden. A couple of assistants were even wrangling Abigail's prized swans into every picture frame.

"Good. Now perhaps a bigger smile." Anton gestured broadly. "I want you to appear radiant with joy. *Radiant*, my Joanna."

She felt about as radiant as a slab of pork, but she dutifully smiled, unsure whether she was conveying the proper amount of joy and really not caring.

During one break while Anton and his assistants reloaded, Margaret, wearing a hat of feathers and ribbon, bustled over to encourage her. "It's going extremely well, Joanna. How are you feeling?"

"I'm getting tired." Stifling her impatience while an assistant added a touch of blush to her cheeks, she asked, "How much longer is this going to take?"

"Anton doesn't feel he's got quite the right picture yet."

"He's already shot three rolls of film, how much more—?" She stopped herself as she heard her voice take on a strident pitch. None of this was Margaret's fault, and taking her own frustrations out on the woman would not be fair. "I'm sorry, Margaret."

The other woman laughed with sympathy and understanding. "My dear, don't worry about it for a moment. I've never had a bride who wasn't a bundle of nerves this close to her wedding."

"Glad to know I'm normal." To cover the irony she hadn't been able to keep from her voice, Jo bent her head to straighten the cuff of one sleeve.

"We were really lucky to get Anton on such short notice. He actually canceled a booking so he could be here today. He said he'd never forgive himself if you had to settle for a second-rate photographer."

Jo's lips quirked. "What that man needs is more self-confidence."

"He's a perfectionist. It's why he's the best."

"Yes, of course." Besides being extremely unfair to Margaret, being cranky about the ordeal would do no good.

"My dear, your gown is simply exquisite. I should have known I had no cause to worry about you of all people having your wedding gown in time. You look absolutely lovely."

"Thank you." She tugged upward on the off-the-shoulder neckline of the dress, but in the end, gave up the effort. It wasn't outrageously low. It also wasn't the gown she would have designed for herself, but it would do fine.

Connie had chosen well, as she had known she would.

"Joanna," Anton called. "I'm all set. Let's take a few more."

"A *few* more what? *Rolls?*"

He laughed. "You know me too well."

"I should. You've taken all my graduation pictures—"

"*Portraits*, my dear. I don't take pictures, I take *portraits*."

"Of course. You've taken all my portraits from elementary school through college, and each time you nearly drove me crazy."

He brought his fingers to his lips and kissed them, making the gesture pure drama. "Trying to capture you on film is torture for me, Joanna. You are so beautiful, no camera can do you justice." He paused to consider his last statement, then added, "Except mine, of course."

"Uh-huh. Right. Just take the pictures, Anton."

"Very well. We will begin again." His eyes narrowed as he studied her. "Joy didn't work that well for us, so I want to try pensive and demure, and it would really be perfection if we could also get ethereal. Tilt your head down and slightly to the left and lower your eyes, as if you are thinking of your beloved, the man you are about to marry, the man you love."

The man she loved—Cale.

No, not love. Emotions of lust and desire definitely zinged between them. And there *was* some sort of connection that enabled him to finish her sentences and her to know that he would seek her out. And there was more. But if it was love she felt for him, surely she would tell him about Kylie, wouldn't she? And she would break her engagement to Brett, wouldn't she?

"Joanna. Hello. Are you with me, dear?"

"Sorry." Angling her head downward as he had asked, she tried to figure out why Cale's name had popped into her mind. Anton had told her to think of the man she loved, and she had thought of Cale. But she wasn't in love with him. No, being in love with him wasn't possible. Just because she thought about him all the time and wanted to be with him. . . .

"Joanna, my darling, concentrate. I want softness in your face, I want radiant expectation, I want full-blown love."

"Yes, Anton."

Hours before, without giving herself time to rethink her decision, she had finally admitted she wanted him as much as he wanted her. Only Kylie's appearance had stopped them from making love.

She was all too aware that she might be stepping from mud into quicksand. A week before her wedding wasn't the time, nor her aunt's estate where all the wedding preparations were going on the place to have an affair. It didn't seem to matter to her or to him, though.

But love? No. Love didn't happen that easily or that quickly, or under these circumstances. She didn't love Cale. She couldn't. Cale . . .

"There," she heard Anton say as the shutter on his camera whirred. "That's much better. In fact that's *marvelous*. Nothing's more lovely than a portrait of a woman in love."

A woman in love. She jerked.

"No, no, *no*!" Anton cried. "Don't move. You had it just right. Concentrate. *Concentrate*."

She deliberately stepped out of the frame. "I'm sorry, but that's all I can do. Use whatever you have."

Throwing up his hands, the photographer wheeled toward his sympathetic assistant. "What have I done to deserve such a fate? I don't have the right shot yet. I don't have *any-thing* really. My reputation is going to be ruined. People will think I am no longer brilliant. I will never get another commission. I will . . ." He dropped his face into his hands and began to loudly sob.

Margaret hurried over. "Joanna, what are you doing? You've upset Anton terribly."

"I'm sorry, Margaret, but you and I both know he's got more than enough shots. We also know that he pretends to cry at least once every session, sometimes more." She raised her voice. "Anton, you did wonderfully as always, and I know you'll pick the absolute right one. Thank you." To Margaret, she said, "I can't do this anymore. I'm going for a walk."

"But—"

She put a reassuring hand on her shoulder. "Margaret, it's nerves, just as you said. And I can't stand here a minute more. But you're not to worry. You're doing a fine job, and everything is getting done. If you need me, you can reach me later on this afternoon. I'll be in my studio."

She turned and blindly headed away from the group gathered in the garden and if possible away from her own thoughts.

"No, wait! Your dress!" Margaret rushed after her. "You can't go for a walk in your dress. It'll be ruined. Aren't you going to change?"

She swept the veil off her head and half tossed, half shoved it toward the other woman, then shot a glance at an anxiously hovering assistant. "Would you please detach the train? Margaret, quit worrying. If my dress gets dirty, I'll have it cleaned." She ignored the other woman's gasp and when the train was removed, she simply walked away, ignoring the questions thrown after her.

She didn't know where she was going, but

she badly needed space to breathe, privacy away from inquiring eyes, quiet from everything going on in her mind. The top layer of her dress was made of light-as-air silk. As she moved it floated over the layers of illusion net and taffeta underskirts, its hem trailing the ground. She wound her way through garden after garden, filled with tulips and daffodils, hyacinth and jonquils, fragrance and color, keeping to the paths when she could and when she couldn't, not worrying about it. Because try as she might, she couldn't get away from her thoughts.

Everything had always been so simple. She'd grown up secure in the knowledge that she was unconditionally loved and buffered from the world by her family. Their position and power meant nothing extraordinary to her. It was her normal.

But even as a young girl she had been able to understand that in many ways she had it easier than most people. And she also understood that in other ways she had it much harder. The Damarons had been cursed and blessed, and sometimes it seemed they were more cursed than blessed. Everything happened to the members of her family on a larger-than-life scale. They couldn't grieve or rejoice privately. They could hide neither their triumphs nor their tragedies from the world. And when one of them did something wrong, the consequences could be monumental.

Now Kylie had done something terribly wrong, and there was no question that she would have to pay some kind of price. She just wanted to be sure Kylie was strong enough and that the price she paid was the *correct* price.

She'd been trying in every way she could think of to protect Kylie—her reaction had been instinctive and immediate. But she also had to figure out how to both protect her and at the same time see that justice was done.

Abruptly she struck out across a meadow, carpeted with wild violets and interspersed with pale pink and light blue forget-me-nots. In some places the grass and wildflowers were close to knee-deep.

She knew where she was going now, a place she had gone to often after her parents had been killed, a glade where a clear brook flowed over rocks and stones, smoothing them, polishing them. Trees grew along its banks, their branches providing shade, and flowers grew as wild as the occasional deer that came to drink.

After a while she passed through an opening in a natural fence of crimson azaleas and pink flowering dogwood. And amid ferns and wild lilies, she dropped down to the ground.

She was there when sometime later Cale came upon her, pensive, still, her hands folded in her lap as she gazed toward the bubbling brook.

Her dress billowed out around her, a luminous circle of white silk. The back of her dress dipped down to a couple of inches above her waist, revealing her straight spine and skin that gleamed with the luster of satin. She'd worn her hair up in a sophisticated coil that looked too heavy for her slender neck. No wonder the photographer had had such a hard time capturing her, he thought. She looked like an exquisite and rare flower amid the natural, uncultivated state of the glade.

"The wildly dramatic Anton should have followed you here with his camera," he said quietly. "He could have gotten his pensive pictures."

She lifted her face to him. "You were watching us?"

She didn't appear surprised to see him. In fact she seemed somewhat relaxed. "Part of the time, enough for me to see that your heart wasn't in it." Pushing aside a billow of white silk, he came down close beside her.

She didn't protest, nor did she look at him. "I don't like having my picture taken. Never have."

"Why's that?"

She shrugged. "I don't know. Maybe the camera *does* steal your soul." She looked down at her hands. "I do know that a photographic image doesn't always tell the truth."

There was a weariness about her he hadn't seen before. "I know what you mean. Anton wanted you to portray a serenely happy bride-to-be. In my estimation you're anything but."

She was quiet for several moments. "What are you doing here, Cale?"

"It's my job to protect you. I needed to know where you were." He paused. "What are *you* doing here?"

She glanced around her. "This glade is one of my favorite places. It's peaceful, and it relaxes me. I found it shortly after Kylie and I moved in with Abigail, right after our parents were killed. I always felt as if nothing bad could happen to me here."

"Were you afraid that something would?"

She shrugged. "After the plane crash I didn't know what to be afraid of. At times even shadows seemed ominous. Something beyond my control, or maybe even someone, had taken my parents away from me, killed them."

"It's an understandable reaction."

"Is it?"

Her eyes were bottomless, unguarded, and he could see past defenses, past pretense until he caught a glimmer of her soul, its purity, its honesty, its fear. He proceeded cautiously, not wanting to spoil the moment. "To have your parents taken away from you so abruptly and so violently would be hard for *anyone* to understand, no matter what age." His expression was drawn with tenderness as he smiled at her. "My parents are alive, but I've always felt responsible for the people around me, especially those I love, my family, my friends."

She searched his face, looking for an answer she didn't know the question to. "Do you ever get over that feeling? That feeling that you have to protect the vulnerable ones?"

He chuckled lightly. "I never have. I'm actually pretty hopeless in that regard. I can't seem to help myself."

Tilting her head, she gazed at him. "You're not talking about a president, are you?"

"When I was a kid, I had a cocker spaniel puppy named Danny. He was my best friend. He went everywhere with me. The day he fell through a thin patch of ice on a frozen lake, I didn't hesitate to jump in after him. And of course it didn't take long before I was in trouble. My shoes, jacket, and several layers of clothes quickly became saturated and weighted me down, but I refused to let go of Danny until help arrived."

Her eyes widened. "You could have drowned."

He grinned. "Yeah, and I almost did. As it was, I suffered a bad case of hypothermia."

"I bet your mother was beside herself."

"Yes. Just like she was the time I climbed a

neighbor's tree with the intention of helping one of my sisters down. And after I got her safely on her way to the ground, I fell out of the tree and broke my arm."

She laughed. "Sounds like you were a handful."

"Unfortunately for Mom so were my sisters. When I was ten I saved one of my sisters from drowning. She was five and was reaching for a toy in the swimming pool when she toppled in. I jumped in after her and found her sitting calmly on the bottom of the pool, waiting for me. Afterward she told Mom she had known I would come and save her." He paused. "So you see, I do understand the need to protect."

She nodded. They seemed to have that need in common, and he would understand, as he seemed to understand so many other things. But she had confidences to keep, a sister to save.

"So who are you trying to protect, Jo?"

From one heartbeat to the next she retreated from him. Oh, it was nothing obvious, more a subtle gathering of her emotions and drawing them into herself so that she was once again protected and shielded. And as easy and as quickly as that he lost the tentative emotional connection he had made with her.

Stifling a sigh, he said, "You're ruining your wedding gown."

She absently smoothed her hand over the skirt. "It's not ruined."

"I remember my sisters' wedding dresses. They were each encased in protective bags and hung carefully on the back of their closet doors until their wedding day. No one was allowed to even breathe on them."

"Your sisters sound very nice, very normal, but everyone is different, and the dress will be fine."

"It's . . ." His fingers brushed across a cluster of pearls on her sleeve, then fingered a line of beads and sequins at the neckline. "I hate it." He saw surprise flash across her face. "I hate it because you're going to marry another man in it."

"*Another* man?" Did he mean as opposed to *him*? The thought caused her heart to skip a beat.

He shook his head. "Any man."

Her brow knitted. "Why do you care who I marry in this dress? I thought all you wanted was to make love to me—have an affair, one of relatively short duration, I might add."

It was a valid observation, he reflected, but one that was quite contradictory to the way he was feeling at the moment. "You're right. But you and I haven't even gotten started yet, and there isn't much time left before you'll be walking down the aisle." Something flickered in and out of her eyes. Was it fear again? "Jo?"

"What?"

"Why are you marrying Brett?"

"I'm sick of that question, and for the last time, I won't discuss it with you."

She didn't simply retreat, she froze up on him. He put his hand on her shoulder and lightly massaged the knotted muscles beneath the silken skin. She didn't resist, but neither did she soften. Her scent was light and fresh and mingled with the scents of the grass and the flowers. He shifted closer, inhaled deeper, then pressed a kiss to the base of her throat where her pulse beat steadily. He kept his mouth there, occasionally flicking out his tongue to taste her until he felt her pulse skip a beat, then flutter, then begin to race. His own pulse rate matched hers, beat for beat; his loins swelled, throbbed, a demanding urgency gripped him.

"Cale?" Her voice was so soft, it was almost carried away by the breeze. "What are you doing?"

He raised his head and reached to pull a pin from her hair, then another, then another. Heavy arctic-blond coils tumbled free. "I'm not waiting any longer, that's what I'm doing."

Pleasure shivered through her with each brush of his fingers against her skin. The heated energy and sexual intensity of his nearness had shattered the peaceful atmosphere she had been enjoying. But there was no going back. Her senses were all focused on him now.

"What's the matter?" he asked, winding a strand of her hair around his finger. "You can't be shocked that I want to make love to you now."

No, she wasn't. Yet in many ways everything he did shocked her. And thrilled her. The combination was making it impossible for her to remain aloof to him.

He kissed her neck again, a slow, sensual kiss that had her sucking in her breath with an audible hiss.

"Is it all right?" he murmured, his mouth against her neck.

"Yes. Very much." There was no sense in denying how much she wanted him, because sooner or later her body would give her away. She wanted to make love to him, and now she finally would be able to. Here, there would be no interruptions, no excuses, no pretense. Just two people who from the start hadn't been able to get enough of each other. She couldn't wait. She just had to make sure of one thing first.

With a groan, he trailed his fingers down her throat, then back up again. "Lord, we've wasted too much time. All these days and nights . . ."

"Yes." Her tongue flicked out to moisten her suddenly dry lips and drew his gaze. "Cale?

You said you'd stop following me and prying into my life—right?"

He hadn't, as a matter of fact. He bent to press a light kiss to her lips. "Tell me again why you asked me to agree to that."

"Because it's not right. Because it's not part of your job description. Because I don't like it. Because I want you to stop."

"All of that, huh?" He laughed softly.

She felt the breath from his laugh on her skin. "All of that."

"Okay." He pushed her hair aside so that he could press a kiss behind her ear.

With him so close, kissing her, touching her, it was hard to keep her thoughts straight. "Okay?"

"Okay." He sensed some kind of trouble, and no matter what, he intended to follow up on his hunch. If he was wrong, there would be no harm done. On the other hand if he was right, he would move heaven and earth to help.

Her thoughts were clouding with his every kiss, but she knew that even if he hadn't agreed, she wouldn't be able to get up and walk away. He was like a magnet to her. Without force he kept her by his side. His vitality, his heat, his strength, his sexuality—it all hammered at her, seduced her.

"Tell me again that you want me." He leaned closer and lightly crisscrossed his fingers across the bare skin beneath her collarbone. "I want your skin to run with heat when I touch you. I want you to moan and claw and take me as deep into you as you can and then take me deeper."

Heat filled her veins and rushed to every part of her body. Her throat tightened, and quivers of reaction shook her. There was only one thing she could say. "I want you." The words were choked out, but they were audible.

Satisfaction burned in his eyes, and he started to lower her to the ground.

"The dress—"

"I don't give a damn about the dress," he said, his voice a growl as he eased her back amid the wild grass and followed her down. "Do you?"

"No." Excitement and alarm clashed within her as she stared up into his hard, dark eyes. There was a fierceness and an implacability there that she couldn't argue with. She'd never imagined that they would make love on the ground, in a glade, with her in a wedding dress. The dress she would be wearing while exchanging marriage vows with another man. But she couldn't, wouldn't stop what was about to happen. "I'll come to the guest house tonight."

He sensed it was an affirmation on her part of what was taking place in her and accepted it as such. "Yes," he said simply. "You will."

He lowered his mouth to hers. Surprisingly

after the intensity of their anticipation, he didn't rush her. He took his time, molding her lips to his, gently enticing her mouth open, courting her tongue with a seductive dance. And at the same time his hands leisurely stroked over her breasts, learning their shape through the silk of the dress, then going to the sensitive skin just above them, exploring and stroking the susceptible swell, corrupting what minuscule resistance remained in her.

Everything in her was melting away. She could actually feel herself soften and the tension that had been her constant companion for the past couple of weeks dissipate and then change to a new, different type of tension. Slowly, surely she began to respond.

Her mouth opened wider, accepting his tongue deeper, and in the pit of her stomach a fire began to burn. There was nowhere for their affair to lead—but it didn't matter. Time constraints and job demands would see that it would end shortly after it began—but it didn't matter. She'd never indulged in a pursuit that was so clearly about pure sex—but it didn't matter. In fact up until now her sexual experience was limited because of an innate caution —but it didn't matter.

Nothing mattered but this moment, in this glade, with this man.

What she felt with Cale was new, scary, and

at the same time bright and beautiful. And at that moment in time it mattered very much.

Gradually the kisses changed, becoming devastatingly thorough and forcefully possessive. She couldn't stop the moan from escaping her as his hands became more insistent, more demanding, causing her nipples to harden to yearning points.

Her hands lifted to his shoulders. The cloth of his shirt was warmed by the sun, and the muscles beneath it moved and shifted as he caressed and kissed her.

How could something so wrong seem so right? she wondered hazily. Why did *this* one man have the power to make her forget everything—decorum, responsibility, common sense? He made her forget everything but that she wanted him.

He tugged at the bodice, impatient now. "This damned dress." Sliding an arm beneath her back, he half raised her from the ground. "Where's the zipper?"

It was her last chance to say no, her last chance for sanity and sound judgment. The chance slipped away without her even trying to grasp it. "No zipper," she whispered. "Buttons."

He pulled away from her slightly so that he could look down at her. "Shall I rip them open or do you want me to take the time to unbutton them."

"I'll do it."

He eased her into a sitting position. "No, I will." Holding her gaze, he reached around her with one hand and, by feel, tackled the line of buttons. "There's something you need to know, Jo. You may marry another man, but on your wedding night you'll be thinking of me."

Caught and held by the raw need in his voice, the dark desire flaming in his eyes, she could only admit he was right. In a flash she realized that no matter what happened in the future she would always think of him.

The buttons went all the way to her hips but already he had the gown open to her waist. She felt the sun on her back as the buttons surrendered to his dexterity. Of its own volition, the neckline began to slip downward. She didn't try to catch it.

"Another man may be touching you," he said harshly, "but all your life you'll remember the way my hands felt on you. After this afternoon your body is going to be marked. No man will ever possess you as I will today." His eyes were bleak as he lowered her back to the grass.

He pushed the bodice of the dress the rest of the way to her waist and bent his head to draw her nipple into his mouth. Desperately clinging to his shoulders, she lifted her hips up to him, writhing as her belly contracted with passion. She'd never known anything like it before. She was on fire.

Cale was painfully aroused, his control in danger of disintegrating completely, and he didn't know what he should do. He wanted to rip the dress open and enter her with a force that would shake both of them to their teeth. But he also wanted this lovemaking to last for as long as he could, to draw out the pleasure until they were both screaming from it.

Just then she arched against him again and he sucked in a sharp breath. "One way or the other this dress is coming off you." He rolled to the side of her, flipped up the long skirt of the dress and reached for the petticoats.

"Wait." Although she didn't really care what happened to the dress, she somehow knew she should. But she was trembling so badly, she wasn't sure if she could do much of anything. Lifting her hips, she futilely tried to push the petticoats over her hips.

Muttering an oath, Cale knotted the material in his fist and jerked downward. He heard something tear, but he didn't stop. Two more harsh jerks and she was free of the taffeta and tulle layers. Then he went to work on the dress. Since he had only undone the buttons to her waist, the dress resisted being pulled down her hips.

Nearly oblivious to his efforts, she threaded

her hands up into his hair and grasped his head. When she felt fabric rip and buttons pop, she pulled his head down to her so that she could once again feel his mouth on hers. She barely recognized herself, tugging at his clothes, kicking off her dress. She felt totally uninhibited and free.

At last both of them were naked and he came over her. Eagerly she spread her legs, accepting his weight into the cradle of her thighs. His hard, swollen length pressed against the sensitive, moist flesh of her own sex, but he didn't enter her. Instead he nudged her, finding the sensitive nub of her pleasure, then repeating the motion. Every muscle in her body tightened, every nerve flamed, every inch of her skin flushed. Pressure built in her, expanded, by the second becoming more and more unbearable.

She clutched at him, her fingers digging into his shoulders. "Cale, please—"

A rough, deep sound rumbled up from his throat, but he held on to the shredding fragments of his control, waiting, while continuing to move against her without once entering her.

And then it happened. She stiffened, then arched her back off the ground and cried out softly as her climax took her. He held her, staring down at her, drinking in the expression of her wonderment, her release, her ecstasy. He had thought her beautiful before but now she was luminescent. And it was because of him. His heart swelled at the thought. But what shook him to his very bones was the sudden realization that he wanted to be the only one to give her ultimate pleasure. He couldn't stand the idea of another man touching her.

Pushing aside the thought, he held her until her shuddering quieted, smoothing his hand over her brow, murmuring words to her that even he didn't know the meaning of.

His heart was beating so hard, his chest felt ready to explode. He couldn't catch his breath. Need was ruling him along with a desire so strong, his teeth ached with it.

He lifted his hips and thrust hard into her silky depths. She gasped at the sudden invasion, but then quickly wrapped her legs around his hips and joined him in the age-old rhythm of lovemaking. He drove deeply into her again and again. For this space of time she was his. She belonged only to him, no one else. She responded only to him, arching her hips up to him, taking him into her and holding him with a tight, hot grip. She was made only for him.

Knowing he wasn't going to be able to endure much more, he clutched her hips and shoved savagely and deeply into her. She held on with all her might, all the while crying out his name. Then her nails bit into his back as she began to spasm around him. With a shuddering groan he let himself go, convulsing into her, releasing everything that was within him with a power never before experienced until he was empty, exhausted, and completely sated.

SEVEN

Something lightly tickled her face, but Jo couldn't rouse herself to brush it away. She was drifting on a cloud, somewhere between wakefulness and sleep and had no desire to surface from the boneless peace that had her in its grip.

Again something tickled her, this time beneath her nose. She managed to raise her hand and lethargically bat it away.

"Are you going to wake up, sleepyhead?"

And just like that she was fully awake, her eyes wide open. Cale was propped up on one elbow, gazing down at her, an intimate warmth in his eyes, a blade of grass in his hand. His naked long, muscled length was stretched out beside her, one side pressing against her.

He chuckled, a sound of pleasure and lazy amusement that rolled up from his chest. "Either that photo session tired you out more than either of us realized or we were very, very good together. As far as I'm concerned it was definitely the latter."

Embarrassment swept through her. She had just surrendered completely to this man, without inhibitions, without any thought to the consequences. Her first impulse was to flee, but she realized that for the present her body couldn't be relied on to do anything quickly. She closed her eyes, but blocking him from her sight didn't block the truth from her mind. She had wanted him passionately, fervently, and hadn't been able to stop herself from making love with him with complete abandon beneath a blue sky, on a carpet of wild grass and flowers.

It had been so much more than she had expected, more than a simple joining of bodies, more than she could handle, really. Given what was going on in the rest of her life, she wasn't entirely comfortable with the woman she'd been in his arms, a woman with no restraint or control. She couldn't change what had happened, wouldn't if she could—which left her with one option. She had to face the reality and try to minimize the damage.

"Jo?" His hand smoothed over her brow, then came to rest on her middle, his long fingers spreading from one side of her waist to the other and down to her belly. With one hand he

had managed to impose a not-so-subtle domin-
ion over her. "Come on, Jo. Look at me."

She did and spoke before he could. "Cale,
what just happened—"

"Forget whatever you're thinking. I can *see*
the wheels turning in that gorgeous head of
yours and your defense shields coming up."

He was right. She had planned to gloss over
the fact that they had made love and then, as
casually as she could, leave. But she was incapa-
ble of glossing it over. They would make love
again, because she wanted to, *fiercely* wanted to.
Even now her naked body tingled with the
need.

She sat up, reached for her wedding dress
and pulled it against her. Glancing around, she
saw her petticoats in a frothy pile not too far
away, their white layers gently undulating in
the breeze like petals of an exquisite flower.

He lifted his hand to her back and brushed
away pieces of grass. "I like you much better
without the dress."

Heat blossomed in her at his touch, causing
huskiness to weave through her voice as she
spoke. "The dress is going to be a problem."

"So throw it away."

Unconsciously she leaned back, increasing
the pressure and warmth of his hand on her
back. "That would be a little tough to explain,
having my wedding photos made in one dress

and getting married in an entirely different one."

"I have a solution for that too. Don't get married."

Her heart gave a thud against her rib cage. "I have someone who works for me in New York who I can get to come down tomorrow and repair the dress. Her name is Alisha, and she's completely reliable."

"I'm not interested. Why are you ignoring what I said?"

She glanced over her shoulder at him. "I'm not."

His jaw tightened, and he jackknifed upright. "I mean it, Jo. There's no way you can marry Saunders after what just happened between us. No way."

The warmth and musky scent of his skin stimulated her senses, bringing a sharp clarity to their surroundings—the rippling sound of the brook as it flowed through the glade, the murmuring swish of the breeze through the trees, the vibrant orange color of wild lilies, the dark afternoon stubble on his face.

A pebble bit into her bare bottom. She tilted to one side and brushed it away, then looked at him. "Let's not ruin our afternoon together."

"I don't want you to marry Saunders, Jo. I want you to break the engagement. I want us to be able to see each other."

It sounded wonderful, simple, but it wasn't. Giving herself a moment to recover, she tossed the wedding gown over her head and pulled it down around her. Holding the bodice in place, she shifted around to him. "What just happened between us was wonderful, I'm not going to lie to you."

"You *couldn't* lie to me about that. There were times when all I had to do was whisper your name to make you quiver."

"I'm not denying it. And you did much more than whisper my name."

His gaze was diamond-hard. "And I want, I plan, to do even more."

"Okay. What are we disagreeing about? That's what I want to do too." She stroked the back of her hand down the side of his face, not thinking of the tenderness of the gesture, but only that she wanted to touch him. "We have time."

"Really?" he asked with rough sarcasm. "And how do you figure that? When did you last look at a calendar?"

It was a rhetorical question. They both knew it was now only a matter of days until her wedding. "We'll make the most of the time we have left."

Shards of conflicting emotions glittered in his eyes. "I wish I could tell you to go to hell. I wish I could tell you that making love to a woman who's about to marry another man doesn't appeal to me. But the woman is you, and I can't tell you either of those things."

A desolate feeling of helplessness besieged her. "Things can't be any different for us, Cale. Not now."

He gripped her arms and shook her lightly. "Yes, they can. All you have to do is tell Saunders to take a hike."

When she didn't respond frustration furrowed his brow. "Are you going through with the wedding because he's offered you the security of marriage? That can't be important to you."

A brief thought flitted through her mind: He didn't think marriage to a man she loved would be important to her. She dismissed the idea. What he did or didn't think about the subject of marriage wasn't important.

"Cale—"

"And it sure as hell can't be that he's good in bed. You wouldn't have just come apart in my arms if he'd been satisfying you."

Her spine stiffened. "Don't make me regret what happened this afternoon."

"Regret?" He released her. "Hell, I'm just trying to make sense of it."

"You don't have to work so hard at it. It's simple. Forget Brett. Brett has nothing to do with what's going on between you and me."

He started to disagree with her, but then clamped his mouth shut. Dammit, he'd wanted to make love with her and he had. So why wasn't he satisfied? "I want you again."

Desire flared at his low, flat, matter-of-fact statement. With regret she glanced at the sky. The sun had started to lower. "I better get back to the house. Abigail will be home soon, and I told Kylie I'd check on her."

"Your family can do without you for a little while longer." He knew he wasn't being reasonable, but every muscle and nerve in his body was screaming to have her again. It would be almost beyond his ability to let her go before he had sheathed himself inside her silky body and gained relief once more.

"If I don't put in an appearance—"

He jerked her to him, causing the bodice of the dress to slip down her arms to her waist. Her breasts pressed against him, and her nipples nestled into the dark curling hair covering his chest. "You can tell them you were in your studio, working and ignoring the phone."

"What if they go down there looking for me?" It was a fleeting random thought that dissolved as soon as she spoke it.

"I don't care. Do you?"

Mutely she shook her head and with a groan he brought his lips down on hers to drink from her mouth, to saturate himself with her taste and her feel, to drench himself in her scent, to immerse himself once more deep inside her.

Threading her arms around his neck, she went soft both inside and out, weakened by the strength of his desire for her, by the strength of her body's reaction to him. Her head reeled, her senses spun, and she collapsed forward against him. He took her weight and rolled backward to the grass, bringing her down on top of him.

He stretched out his full length and held her there for a long time, his lips exploring hers, his fingers memorizing the valley of her spine. He dipped beneath the open waistline of the dress to mold the irresistible curves of her bottom with his hand and to pull her pelvis harder into his. But the damned dress irritated him.

He was harder than he ever remembered being, with excruciating need throbbing in every part of his body. He didn't want to let her go long enough to completely undress her and with relief he realized he didn't have to. She was completely naked beneath the dress, open to him. There were no barriers between them.

He tore his lips away from hers and pressed his mouth at the hollow behind her ear. "From this moment on," he murmured, "I want you as often as possible."

"Yes," she whispered back. This affair between them wouldn't last long, but while it did she wanted to experience everything. Soon Cale would walk out of her life, but for now, she vowed, she would savor him and their time together.

He bunched the voluminous skirt up around her waist then lifted her hips and brought her down hard on his rigid length, burying himself to the hilt inside the heated, velvet tightness of her body.

She cried out at the sudden sharp spear of ecstasy that pierced through her, followed almost immediately by another and another as he lifted his hips, thrusting urgently, almost violently up into her again and again and at the same time kneading her breasts and rubbing his thumbs across the distended nipples. The feeling was agonizing.

Thrilling waves of rapture crashed over her. Bracing her hands on his chest, she threw back her head and rode him. He filled her completely, touching acutely sensitive pleasure points deep inside her. Helpless, overwhelmed, on fire, she started to cry as her inner spasms began. With a grunt he grasped her hips, pulled her down forcefully on him and convulsed into her, reaching his own powerful release. Holding on tightly to him, she careened over the edge with him.

Jo climbed out of the shower and dried herself off. She had spent a long time beneath the pulsating spray of the water, doing her best to wash Cale's smell from her body. She'd used her favorite scented soap and as soon as she finished drying herself she slathered perfumed lotion over her entire body.

But she could still smell him. Actually she could still *feel* him—his hands on her skin, his hard sex inside her. She didn't think her body would ever be the same. It was as if he had indelibly imprinted himself on her right down to her very bones.

There was nothing she could do about it, she told herself. Nothing she wanted to do about it right now. What energy she possessed had to go elsewhere. She was caught in the sensual web he had spun around her and during the next few days she wasn't going to fight it.

After she'd dressed in a simple gold silk dress that Brett had made a point of telling her was one of his favorites, she walked to her bed to survey the wedding gown she had tossed there as she'd come in the door.

She gave a small prayer of thanks that she'd actually been able to make it into the house without being seen, then with a sigh she shook her head. If she had to rely on anyone else beside Alisha to repair it, she would say the gown was ruined. Pearls and sequins were missing, and threads dangled emptily. There was a two-inch-long rent in a side seam. About a dozen of the silk button loops were ripped apart.

Blotches of grass and dirt dotted the white silk, so many at times they ran together. And, yes, there was even the telltale stain of semen. But once Alisha worked her magic, treating the stains and sewing her invisible stitches—in case anyone asked to see the dress—no one would be able to tell that she had made love in the dress. At least she hoped they wouldn't.

It seemed that Cale's sisters had been on the right track when they had hung their wedding gowns on their closet door and refused to let anyone so much as breathe on them. With another sigh, she scooped up the dress and tossed it into her closet on her way out the door.

Brett was waiting downstairs for her in the sitting room, lounging in the cushioned depths of a chair, enjoying a glass of Abigail's finest brandy.

She closed the door behind her and schooled her voice to neutrality. "Abigail just informed me you won't be staying for dinner."

"That's right." He came to his feet and kissed her lightly.

She barely stifled the urge to wipe her mouth. After an afternoon of Cale's kissing, it seemed profane for her to allow another man to kiss her. Silly of her to feel that way, but true nevertheless. "Do you have a meeting?"

Slipping his arm around her shoulders, he chuckled. "With all your cousins flying in for our wedding, I decided I'd better get my office shipshape. Can I get you something to drink?"

"No, thank you." Casually she stepped from beneath his arms and settled herself on the couch and *tried* not to let it irritate her too much that he was already playing the host in a Damaron house.

He grinned, clearly happy. "I want to impress my new in-laws."

"You've worked for Damaron International for quite a while now. You've already impressed them. Otherwise you wouldn't still be working there."

He dropped back into the chair and sniffed at the brandy. "That's true. But I'm about to become family, and once I do, they'll look at me in a different light. I'm expecting that they'll want to give me much more responsibility, and I plan to be ready."

She nodded dutifully. "I'm sure you will be."

"Oh, there's no question." He gestured with the glass. "And by the way, I expect you to put in a good word for me."

"I'm sure it won't be necessary."

His hand was the only part of him that moved. It tightened around the glass. "But you *will* talk to them about me, won't you? In time I expect to sit on the board."

She took a deep breath. "I will talk to the family about giving you more responsibility, but no one sits on the board who isn't a Damaron by blood. You know that."

His eyes narrowed on her, and he leaned forward. "I know that up until *now* no one sits on the board who doesn't have that famous silver streak in their hair. But I also know that the requirements are about to change. *I* am going to sit on the board, because *you* are going to see to it that I do. Isn't that right, Jo?"

She heard the dangerous edge of his voice and knew what was required of her. "Whatever you say, Brett."

He sat back in the chair, a smile of satisfaction on his handsome face. Swirling the brandy in a languorous fashion, he said, "It was good to see Kylie come down for breakfast this morning."

"Yes, it was."

"I told you she'd come out of her funk, didn't I?"

"It wasn't a funk." Her voice was sharper than she intended, but she couldn't help it. "She's been scared to death."

He shrugged. "I told both of you there was no reason for her to be."

She jumped into the opening he had given her. "But what if it turns out someone saw something?"

"No one did. I told you that. You're going to have to learn to listen to me."

"I don't understand. How can you be so sure?"

His gaze lifted from the brandy. "I'm sure, okay?"

"But what if someone finds the fireplace poker?"

"No one will. It's well hidden, but . . . if I need it, I can get my hands on it quickly." He smiled at her, obviously very pleased with himself. "Now let's talk about our honeymoon."

The honeymoon was the last thing on her mind, and she stifled a groan at the change of conversation. "I thought you wanted to surprise me."

"The location *will* be a surprise to you." His smile widened. "But I thought we might talk about the really important part of our honeymoon, the *sexual* part, and why you're so insistent that we wait."

She lied without compunction. "I'm old-fashioned. I believe sex should be a part of marriage, not part of the courtship."

He placed the brandy on the table beside him and leaned forward, his forearms on his knees. "But we're not in the courtship. We went straight past it to the engagement. And there isn't a couple today that doesn't sleep together during their engagement. Dammit, Jo, I've always wanted you, you know that."

What he had always wanted was to marry into the Damaron family, she reflected cynically. She jumped up from the couch and circled it, instinctively putting its width between the two of them. "We are not having a long engagement. I agreed to a quick marriage. I'm planning our wedding. I've done everything exactly as you wished." Beginning to tremble, she braced her hands on the back of the couch. "The least you can do for me is this one thing. I want to wait until our honeymoon."

He stared at her for a moment, his expression as sharp as cut crystal with the added touch of cruelty. Then he rose and walked toward her, stopping only when his knees hit the edge of the sofa. He was close enough to reach across the width that separated them and touch her. She held her breath, steeling herself not to flinch if he did.

"You want to wait?" he asked, sternly pointing a finger at her. "Okay, we'll wait. But once we've said *I do* this abstinence will come to a screeching halt. I've been a good boy too long, and I'm damn tired of it. I'm ready for rewards, *lots* of them."

"All right, Brett."

"Is anything wrong?" Kylie had stepped into the room and was now looking uncertainly from one to the other.

Brett's mask of civility slipped back into place. "No, of course not. Come in, come in. Your sister was just trying to get our honeymoon location out of me, but I'm determined to keep it as a surprise until we're on our way."

Jo fought down the nausea that rose in her throat.

There would never be a honeymoon.

There would never be a wedding.

Brett would never touch her.

She would see him dead first.

Dinner seemed interminable to Jo, and she had no idea what she put in her mouth. Whatever the cook had served it all tasted the same to her. Luckily Abigail and Kylie were the only other two at the table and she didn't have to put herself out too much. Abigail carried most of the conversation with updates on various members of the family and their imminent arrivals. Even Kylie contributed a comment now and again.

Jo kept a watchful eye on her. To a certain extent Kylie had been emotionally fragile ever since their parents had been killed. But this past week there'd been times when Jo had actually feared for her sanity. Thankfully Kylie was now making an obvious effort to break free of the emotional paralysis that had gripped her since the night of the Seaberg party. Now she had to do her part and not let her down.

By this time she had hoped to have some concrete information that would help both of them. Alvin Shaw had a twenty-four-hour tail on Brett, but so far he hadn't been able to come up with much.

As for herself, she had agreed to everything Brett had asked, with the exception of having sex with him. She had not only acceded to his wishes to marry and rush the wedding, but she had acquiesced to his wish that she be loving to him in public. And she had gone one step further by being as nice as she could stand to be when they were alone. It was her hope that he would be lulled by a false sense of security and let something slip. Unfortunately that hadn't happened. But she still had to continue to let him think he was winning. He might get cocky and brag about his part in that night. And as long as he thought he was winning, he wouldn't be as dangerous to Kylie.

Over the last couple of weeks she'd been alternately furious and frightened out of her mind. But up until now she had been positive she would be able to find out what she needed to know before the wedding so that she wouldn't have to marry him. Tonight, however, she wasn't so sure anymore.

Cale was on one side of her and Brett was on the other side, both pressuring her. And even though each man was exerting a different type of pressure, she felt trapped.

For the first time she was beginning to doubt her ability to help Kylie, and her fear was growing exponentially. There was so little time left and so much riding on the outcome. Something had to break soon.

When dinner ended she waited until Abigail and Kylie retired to their rooms, then left the house by a back door and started out across the lawn. The decision to go to Cale after dinner had not been a conscious one, but instinctive—especially after the meeting with Brett.

The moon was bright, and the night was clear with the fragrances of night-blooming flowers in the air. She saw no one as she made her way to the guest house. The security on the actual grounds of the estate would be stepped up once the family began arriving in a few days, but until then all was quiet. She was glad. No one would understand why she was going to Cale in the dead of night; she wasn't even sure she understood.

As she drew nearer to the small house she could see no light on, and the fact gave her pause. Was it possible that he'd already gone to sleep? What if he wasn't even there? He could have elected to go into town for the night, or back to his own home. Wherever it was. Odd, but she didn't even know.

Emotionally she'd opened herself up to him more than she ever had to any man. She'd allowed herself to let go of the tight hold she

usually held on herself and to fully feel. And
just the memory of it made her heartbeat accel-
erate as she climbed the steps to the porch.

"What kept you?"

Cale's voice came to her out of the darkness.

"I had dinner with Abigail and Kylie."

He reached for her and pulled her against
him. "I was hungry, too, but I waited for you."

Before she could say anything, he bent his
head and pressed his mouth to hers in a long,
deep, lingering kiss. By the time he lifted his
head, she was trembling with desire.

"I'll honestly do the best I can to be with
you as often as possible," she whispered, "but I
can't do anything to jeopardize my family or
my relationship with Brett."

He cursed. "Saunders can go straight to
hell, and as for you, if I don't make love to you
this minute, I may have to do something dire."

"Dire?"

"Never mind," he muttered, and swept her
up into his arms and carried her into the house
and the bedroom.

There on the bed, they stripped off their
clothes and came together. So natural, so easy,
Jo thought moments later, laving her tongue
along his abdomen, educating herself on the
planes of his body, the intriguing little dips, the
fascinating sensation of his shifting muscles,

the mesmerizing quality of his different textures.

At the side of his waist, she sucked his skin, tasting him, feeling him. She did the same thing at his inner thigh, tugging on small parts of him, nibbling, savoring. Then she made her way higher to a place that had an entirely different shape and form. Soft, sensitive. Hard, throbbing. She partook of it all. Greedily. Enthusiastically.

Shudders shook his body. With a groan he threaded his fingers into her hair and held her head to him. His chest burned as his breath rasped in and out, the sound so loud, it filled the room. Everything in him was screaming for release, but she kept upping the quotient of pleasure, increasing the pressure that was building in him. His need for her was both ferocious and frightening. No woman had ever been able to turn him inside out with such unbearable craving as she was doing. She filled every part of him. He was going to explode any second now, and he had the strange feeling that when he did, there might be nothing left of him but her.

Her hair trailed across his stomach as she changed positions, then she began to lick her way up his torso, taking her time, her tongue leaving a trail of heat and moisture. When she finally reached his mouth, he couldn't wait a moment longer.

With a grunt he wrapped his arms and legs around her and rolled over with her, pinning her to the mattress with his weight. Without preamble he parted her thighs, positioned himself, and drove into her.

He was thinking only of himself. He had never before treated a woman like this, putting his needs first. But Jo had made him too hungry, too hard, too needy. There was a vague thought in his mind that he would make it up to her later, bringing her to her own climax once he'd had his. But for now his control was nonexistent, and he was nothing but raw nerves and hot desire.

Incredibly his urgency grew. His hips flexed, and he hammered harder into her. As much as his body hungered for its deliverance, it was as if it didn't want to let her go. Madness. Ecstasy.

Suddenly he stiffened, threw back his head and cried out as his release gripped him. At the same instant, her inner muscles started to work, milking him. He barely had a split second to be amazed at their physical synchronicity, and then his climax overcame him, and it was all the more powerful because it was shared with her.

Jo awoke as the first light of dawn began to steal through the slats of the shutters. Cale lay beside her, sleeping, his breathing deep and even, his body warm and musky.

She wasn't in his arms, but she had been most of the night. More than once she remembered waking to find herself held tightly against him. Twice she awoke to find him inside her, fully aroused, with her already responding and shivering with delight. It had been a remarkable night, a memorable night.

She eased over on her side so that she could watch him. Even asleep he exuded an animal sexuality that reached out to her. Maybe it was his size, or the strength and fitness of his body. Or maybe it was simply the way her eyes and heart saw him. She had a dilemma.

What did she know about him? That he was persistent. That he had two sisters, parents still living, and a couple of degrees from MIT. That he could sense something wrong when other people couldn't. That he was compelled to protect people—heads of state, his sisters, puppies, her. That from the first he had known how to kiss her and touch her to make her forget everything else. That he could infuriate her and at the same time make her breathless with desire. That he drew her as no other man ever had. That if it were possible, she would spend every minute of the day and night with him.

That she loved him.

She squeezed her eyes shut, and a tear slipped from beneath her lashes. She loved him. It seemed impossible, but there it was. The thought that had first occurred to her yesterday during the photo session was actually true. She loved him.

After several moments she quietly slipped from the bed, dressed, and left.

EIGHT

Jo's gaze blurred on the order form, one of about fifty, that had been faxed to her from New York that morning. In addition to everything else that had been going on in her life, she had been doing her best to stay on top of her business. Today her effort was futile. She'd been staring at the same form for the last fifteen minutes.

She pushed the whole stack away and grabbed a pencil and a sketch pad. She had always thought better with a pencil in her hand, whether she was sketching or simply doodling. But after a few minutes she realized that her mind was still a blank and all she seemed able to do was doodle endless, meaningless spirals.

She threw the pencil down and rubbed her face. Abigail's home had been a haven for her and Kylie the last thirteen years. After she'd left to move to New York to start her business, she had built the studio here, not as a retreat, but as a place to stay in touch with her work when she came home. Today, however, she was definitely retreating.

Hours before she had admitted to herself that she loved Cale. Realizing that she was in love should have been one of the happiest times of her life, but the knowledge had struck her as incredibly sad.

Her life was impossibly complicated, and at the moment she could see no way to untangle it. Plus—and this was an enormous plus—Cale didn't love her. Once his job was over, he wouln't be sticking around. He would take whatever he wanted from her, and he would leave.

Kylie stuck her head through the open doorway. "Am I disturbing you?"

Jo jerked around in surprise. "Goodness no. What are you doing here? Is something wrong?"

Kylie made herself comfortable on a stool on the other side of the drafting table from where Jo sat. "You mean more than usual? No. I just thought I'd walk down here and find you. I hadn't seen you yet today."

"I'm sorry, honey." She pointed to the phone. "All you had to do was call."

"I know." She frowned. "But I thought I'd like to talk to you . . . face-to-face."

"About what?"

"I was wondering . . ."

"Yes?"

"Last night . . . when I walked in on you and Brett, the atmosphere seemed, I don't know, a little tense. Is something wrong between you two?"

"No, of course not."

"Are you sure? Because . . . during the time I spent up in my room, I, uh, sort of wondered about you and Brett." She made an attempt at a laugh, but only partially succeeded. "At least I did when I wasn't thinking about myself."

Jo reached across the table and grasped her hand. "Honey, after what you've been through I don't blame you for worrying about yourself."

"I know you don't. I also know you're carrying a huge burden because of me, and you've been wonderful, never once complaining. Neither has Brett." She looked at Jo. "He hasn't, has he?"

"No, he hasn't." Jo sat back and stared at the doodles she had drawn.

"Jo?"

"What honey?"

"You do love Brett, don't you?"

She hadn't told her sister anything about Brett's blackmail. By the time he approached her the day after the party, she was already having a hard time keeping Kylie from spinning completely out of control. Then hadn't been the time, nor was now.

"I'm marrying him, aren't I?" She'd given much the same answer to Cale, she remembered, though he hadn't bought it.

"Ever since that night I've been completely wrapped up in myself," Kylie said pensively. "I've been moving in a fog, and I sure haven't been thinking straight. But it finally occurred to me a little bit ago that you announced your engagement right after that night. Jo, I didn't even know you were seeing him."

"Well, I had been from time to time whenever we both happened to be in the city at the same time." The fact that it was always business when she saw him she kept to herself. She was better at withholding information than she was at outright lying. "What is it you're worrying about?"

"Lord, Jo, why don't you ask me what I'm *not* worrying about. It'd be easier to answer."

"I know." Jo rubbed her eyes. "Listen, Sin and Jonah and the rest will be here soon. Please—"

The color drained from Kylie's face, and abject horror instantly sprang into her eyes. "Jo, you *promised*! You said you wouldn't tell them!"

"But honey—"

"No! No!" Kylie shook her head frantically. "I couldn't take it if they knew. I couldn't!"

"Kylie, just listen to me. I've tried to tell you—they'd understand. You think they haven't made mistakes? Everyone has."

"Not like this one."

"Probably worse."

"If they have, I've never heard about it."

"Honey, they love you, and they would move heaven and earth to help you. How can you not know that?"

"I do know it—don't you think I do?" Tears sprang into her eyes. "But they've always been able to handle anything. They never would have done what I did, and they'd hate me if they knew." Her voice broke on a sob.

"*I* don't hate you, and I know."

"You're my sister."

"And they're your cousins, your family." It was the same conversation almost verbatim she had had with Kylie right after the party. She hadn't gotten through to her then, but she had hoped she would have a better chance now. The problem was Kylie *idolized* her cousins and couldn't bear the thought that they might think badly of her.

Kylie pointed a shaking finger at her. "If you tell Sin and the others, I will leave here and you will never see me again. I can do it. I'll walk out the front door, and I won't care where I end up."

It was the same threat that had prompted Jo to promise her she wouldn't tell the family what had happened. There had been many times she'd considered breaking the promise, but she had kept quiet. Among other things she wasn't sure what her cousins could do that she wasn't. Except perhaps kill Brett, which was extremely likely. In fact they might band together and do it en masse. But she wasn't ready to have two or more people in her family charged with murder, and she also couldn't risk Kylie leaving.

"Okay, sweetheart. I won't break my promise, but I do need to ask you a few things."

Kylie's horror dwindled to simple fear and wariness. "What?"

"About that night." She was also praying Kylie would remember something now that she hadn't then.

"Why? I thought Brett had taken care of everything."

"He did, he did." Damn, but this was so hard. She didn't want her sister to worry any more than she already was, yet she needed her help. Up until now Kylie had been in no shape for her to question very hard, and there were times she was convinced that any kind of additional pressure would send her over the edge. But the truth was she had waited about as long as she could. "I just want to get things perfectly straight in my mind about what happened, that's all." Kylie groaned. "I know this is hard for you, but I want to make sure that we haven't overlooked anything."

Kylie exhaled a long breath. "I'm sorry I'm giving you so much trouble, Jo. I know you're only trying to take care of things like you always have, and I appreciate it, believe me."

"I do." She mustered a smile. "So, okay, stick with me on this. Now, that night during the party you decided you wanted some air, and so you ducked out onto the terrace and you found Glen out there."

"That's right. He was coming in the back way. He told me he'd just arrived."

"That must have been why no one at the party saw him."

"I guess, and once he and I started talking, he didn't seem to be in much of a hurry to go in, even though he was definitely in the party mood. He was higher than a kite."

"Do you know what he'd taken?"

"I only know what he offered me. Cocaine."

This was the second time she had heard Kylie's version of that night, but she still had to bite her lip to keep from screaming at her sister. Kylie should have known better than to be around any kind of drugs. But she'd not only been around them, she'd gone one step further and taken them. "And so you went down to the pool house with him so that you could do cocaine."

Keeping her eyes cast downward, Kylie nodded. "It was the first time I'd ever tried any drugs, and when it hit my system, it was the wildest sensation I'd ever experienced. But I'd give anything now if I'd never seen it or Glen."

Nausea rose in Jo's throat. Kylie had been incredibly stupid, and she would pay for it for the rest of her life. But being judgmental at this point wouldn't help a thing. Even though Kylie was taking one step forward, she at times would take two steps back. She *was* making an effort though, and it was her job to keep her going forward. "And then what happened?"

"Certain things aren't really that clear after that. I'd already had a couple of drinks before the cocaine, and the combination must have hit me hard, but I do remember Glen started coming on to me. I kept telling him no, but it was like he couldn't hear me."

"So he wouldn't stop?"

"He kept grabbing at me, and he started tearing at my clothes. I got scared. I panicked. I couldn't seem to control either him or me." Tears choked her.

She gave Kylie a moment to collect herself while she did the same. They were about to get to the part that had been giving Jo nightmares and filling her every waking moment with guilt.

"Okay, so that's when you picked up the fireplace poker?"

"Yes." Kylie wiped at her eyes. "No. What fireplace poker?"

"The fireplace poker you hit Glen with." Kylie fell silent.

"Honey? Don't you remember?"

"I thought I remembered. I remember the fireplace, but I don't remember a poker."

"Then what did you use to hit him with?"

"A cue. You know—a pool cue. The Seabergs have a pool table in their pool house. He backed me up to the table and was coming down on me. He was so heavy, and his breath stank. I reached for the nearest thing I could find. A pool cue that was lying on the table. I'm not proud of it, but . . . Jo, what's wrong?"

She stared at her, stunned. "I thought you told me you'd hit him with a poker."

Kylie shook her head. "I can't remember what I told you. I was pretty hysterical when I was telling you."

She was right, Jo realized. She had been crying so hard that night when she'd gotten home that she had been able to tell her only the basic facts—cocaine, Glen coming on to her, she'd killed him. It had been *Brett* who had mentioned the poker. How could he have mistaken a pool cue for a fireplace poker? Kylie wouldn't have had the strength to kill a man with a pool cue.

Perhaps this inconsistency would help her figure out what had actually happened. She'd always believed there had to be more to the story. It was that belief that had kept her going.

"But you saw Glen fall, right?"

Tears rushed back into her eyes. "Yes. He stumbled backward, clutching his head. And there was blood. And then he fell. And then he didn't move again."

"What happened next?"

"Brett came in and told me to leave. That he'd take care of it. Jo, why all the questions days after the fact? Does it have something to do with you and Brett?"

"I was just trying to get things straight. Like I said, I don't want any loose ends left dangling."

Kylie dropped her head in her hands. "Poor Glen. If he hadn't been so high, he would never have come on to me like he did. But whatever he did, he didn't deserve to die."

"He would have raped you, Kylie, if you hadn't stopped him."

"But I didn't mean to *kill* him." Kylie began to cry in earnest.

Jo slid off her stool and went to comfort her sister, putting her arms around her slight figure and hugging her close. "I know you didn't. If you did kill him, it was an accident."

"But it doesn't matter whether it was an accident or not, does it? He's still dead, and his poor parents need to know that he's dead so that they can bury him and mourn him properly."

"I know." She'd been wrestling with the same thing. She'd hoped that she could talk Brett into telling her where he'd buried Glen's body and then somehow get the information to the police without incriminating Kylie. But so far she'd been miserably ineffective.

Cale walked down the path toward the studio with only one thing on his mind—seeing Jo. Ever since he'd awakened to find her missing from his bed, he'd been as irritable as a bear with a sore paw, so much so he'd caught a couple of his men looking at him strangely. He didn't blame them; he was clearly not himself. He felt like an addict who needed a fix.

He strolled through the open door, but the sight of Jo comforting her sister brought him to a stop. "What's wrong?"

Both women started at the sound of his voice. Jo threw a reassuring smile at Kylie before she drew away from her. "Cale? What are you doing here?"

He slipped his hands into his trouser pockets and ambled forward. "Oh, I just came by to check up on a few details. Is something wrong?" He looked at Kylie. "Can I help?"

"No"—she glanced at Jo as if for guidance—"thank you."

"Jo?"

"It's nothing, Cale. Just emotions running high before the wedding."

With a smile he drew a handkerchief from his pocket, leaned closer to Kylie, and gently dabbed her face. "I understand about young girls and emotions. I grew up with two sisters, Kylie. Everything was a drama. If one of them couldn't find their hairbrush, it was a drama. If I happened to say *good morning* the wrong way, it was a drama."

She looked at him blankly.

Cale's smile stayed in place, even though her reaction wasn't quite what he'd been expecting. "More than a lost hairbrush, huh?" His voice was soft. "Maybe a fight with your boyfriend? Just give me his name," he said with mock seriousness, "and I'll go have a talk with him."

Though he didn't know it, Jo thought as she watched them both, the teenage dramas of his sisters couldn't begin to compare with what Kylie was going through. But she found the fact that he was trying with her sister endearing, and she was grateful for the effort. "She's going to be fine. As you know she hasn't been feeling well, and she's probably tried to do too much too soon."

He frowned. True, Kylie didn't exactly look

like the picture of health. He reached out and touched the young girl's cheek in a gentle, yet teasing manner. "I'm sure your sister is right. But keep in mind that I'm always on call. I'm terrific with wayward boyfriends, and I have two excellent references to prove it."

Her smile was reserved. "Thank you. Jo, I'm going to head back to the house. I'll see you later?"

"You sure will. I'll be up for lunch."

Kylie nodded. "See you then."

Jo waited until her sister had left then turned to him. "Do you really have two sisters or are they invented and you make up stories about them as needed?"

He chuckled. "Trust me. No one could invent my sisters. They're true originals."

"Well, if they're indeed real, I think they're pretty lucky to have a big brother who loves them so much."

"Just like Kylie is lucky to have you." He paused, studying her face for clues, not particularly caring what kind of clues he found.

Any kernel of knowledge about what was going on inside her would do. The two of them had shared incredible intimacy, but it had been an intimacy of the flesh. He still didn't have too much of an idea what went on in her head, and it bothered the hell out of him. She was complicated, sexy, difficult, sensual, beautiful, and she was driving him crazy. "It must have been something pretty big that upset Kylie. I purposely didn't ask her if she'd called Lieutenant Robinson. Has she?"

"She will soon."

"That's what you've been saying."

"So?"

"So she needs to do it."

"And she will. Soon." In hopes of diverting him, Jo smiled. "Look, don't take it too personally that you couldn't get through to her. Now and then you're bound to run into one or two young girls who won't automatically fall under the spell of your charm."

Talk about spells, he thought ruefully. Her smile was capable of working a first-class incantation. "I wanted to help."

Her smile faded in the face of his obvious sincerity. "I know you did. You instinctively tried to reach out to Kylie, and I appreciate it. Most men would run the other way at the first glimpse of a young girl's tears."

"I told you. I have a lot of experience with—"

"I know, I know. Your sisters. What are their names, anyway?"

"Rachel and Roberta—Rach and Robbie. They're twins."

"Twins?" She tried to imagine him as a protective older brother and succeeded. He would have been a great brother. Still was, she was sure.

His expression changed. "And now that we've discussed our respective sisters I'd like to get to what I came here for."

"Which is?"

He had her in his arms and was kissing her before she could draw her next breath. And then she forgot all about breathing. After all, oxygen couldn't live in a fire.

But she still tried to hold back, afraid he would discover the secret she had just learned herself, the secret she was determined to keep, the secret of her heart.

"What's wrong?" he asked, releasing her.

She reached behind her for the drafting table to steady herself. "You kiss me and then ask me what's wrong?" She laughed shakily, her blood still simmering from his kiss. "Sorry, but I don't get the connection."

"Something has happened between the last time I saw you and now. Something's different."

She eased around the drafting table and sank onto the stool, grateful to have something solid beneath her. He had to be guessing, she told herself. No one was *that* intuitive. No one outside the family was that attuned to her. "As I remember the last time you saw me we were in bed, and nothing happened except that I got up."

"And *left*. When I woke up this morning, you were gone."

"I didn't see any reason to disturb you, and I thought it best to get back to the house before everyone got up."

What she said made perfect sense. So why had he been so upset to find her gone? "Next time, wake me."

"All right." There was no point in playing coy and qualifying her answer by saying *if* there was a next time. They both knew there would be.

"Did Saunders come for breakfast this morning?"

"You know he didn't. You're notified when anyone sets foot on or off this estate."

"Not anyone. Just Saunders. I seem to have a special interest in him."

"I guess having an affair with a man's fiancée will do that to you." His eyes narrowed on her. She sighed. "I'm sorry. I didn't mean to sound quite so sarcastic."

"Don't be sorry. You're right. I did know he hadn't come for breakfast. I asked because he's on my mind. In fact I can't get him out of my mind. He bothers the hell out of me." He gave a lopsided grin. "I keep seeing him as one of those little groom figures on top of a wedding cake, and then I see a giant fist coming down on top of him and smashing him into the cake." He looked at his hand. "The fist looks remarkably like mine."

She couldn't help it. She giggled.

"Doesn't take Freud to figure that one out, huh?" He came around behind her and began to lightly massage her shoulders. "Tense," he murmured, "very tense, and I can understand why." Beneath his fingers her muscles tightened even more.

"You can?"

"I wouldn't imagine that you're used to duplicitous behavior."

"No, I'm not." To make it worse on her the duplicity was being played out on several levels.

"So dump Saunders." He pulled her to her feet and turned her to him, serious again. "*Dump* him, Jo."

She exhaled heavily. "We've already been through this."

"But you keep sidestepping the issue."

The urge to tell him the truth was tremendous. But even though she loved him, she had no idea how he felt about her. Could she trust him? "Brett's *not* something that can be sidestepped." Her voice cracked, half humor, half pain. "You can't go around him, you can't go through him, you can't go over him. He's there, and he's not going to go away. Talking about him is not going to change anything. Accept it."

"No."

She broke away from his hold. "What is it you want from me, Cale?"

"All I'm trying to do is understand how you can make love with me one minute and coolly contemplate marrying someone else the next."

It seemed to her that she gazed at him for a long time while thoughts formed, broke apart, and re-formed in her head. Was it possible he might love her, even a little? "Okay then, you help me understand something. Why are you so against my marrying Brett?"

"Isn't it obvious?"

"No, it's not."

It took all of his self-control not to shout at her. Instead, he replied calmly, if a trifle forcefully. "Because, Jo, it's going to interfere like hell with you and me."

Her heart sank. "Then what you're saying is that you want our affair to continue after the wedding?"

"No," he said, his teeth gritted. "What I'm saying is that I don't want you to get married in the first place."

"Why?" Her hope returned. "What if I told you that there would be a way we could continue our affair after my wedding? Would that make you happy? Would you back off then?"

"Dammit, Jo!"

"What? I'm trying to understand. Help me. What is it you want?"

"I don't share."

It was a simple, bald, basic statement of

possessiveness, and it sent a sharp thrill through her, but he still hadn't given her any idea how he really felt about her. She baited him a little more. "How do you know you're not sharing me now?"

"Because Saunders is never here long enough."

"You know when he arrives and when he leaves, but how do you know what we're doing in between time? The act can take as long as or as little time as one wishes."

His hand shot out to grasp her upper arm and pull her against him. "Tell me you're not letting him touch you."

The intensity and strength of his sudden anger caught her off guard. "Would it really matter to you if I was?"

His mouth tightened, and he released her. "It would just about kill me."

"Why? *Why*, Cale? And don't tell me it's because you don't share."

"I don't want Saunders to have you in any way, shape, or form. Because *I* want you, with more strength and power than I have ever wanted anyone or anything."

Maybe he didn't love her, she thought, but whatever he felt for her, it was powerful. Would it be enough? For him? For her? She wasn't sure. "He doesn't touch me," she said softly, then raised up on her tiptoes and lightly kissed him. "I'm due up at the house. I'll see you soon."

Minutes later he was still staring at the empty doorway, stunned by the force of his own emotions regarding her.

When he'd met her that night in the Caldwells' garden, he'd never expected not to be satisfied with a brief affair. He'd never expected the heartbreak and the emotions that wrenched his gut when he thought of her with another man. He'd never expected the hunger he constantly felt for her, the raw basic need, as if he wasn't whole unless he was with her.

What was he going to do?

One of the household staff handed Jo a portable phone. "For you. A Mr. Shaw."

Her heart pounding with hope, Jo waited until she was alone, then answered. "This is Joanna Damaron. Have you been able to find out anything new?"

"It's taken me a while, but I've finally got Saunders tied in to drugs."

Of all the things she was expecting or even hoping to hear, drugs was the last thing. "Excuse me?"

"Seems he's been making extra pocket change by supplying the kids in your area with recreational drugs. A few are even into the harder stuff, thanks to him."

"Oh, God." She closed her eyes as a sick feeling swept over her. So she and Kylie weren't his only victims.

"And that's not all. One of the kids he was supplying to was Glen Keenan. It seems Glen was pretty heavily into it."

"But if you know this, the police must know it too."

"Not necessarily. I've discovered the kids around your area are a pretty closed clique. They don't snitch on each other. Lucky for me I just happened to cozy up to a girl when she was coming down off a bad trip and didn't feel so good. She was having a crying jag, and I was there to comfort and listen. We got lucky, Miss Damaron."

"Did we?" She wasn't sure how the information could help them. Would reverse blackmail do the trick? Brett wanted to marry into the family so badly, there was a good possibility he wouldn't fall for her bluff. After all, the punishment for dealing drugs was nothing compared to the punishment for murder that Kylie would have to face.

No, what she needed was a miracle.

NINE

Jo hadn't been able to question Kylie at lunch because Abigail was there. But later that afternoon she found her in her room, propped up against a big square pillow, sitting on the window seat, a book in her lap.

"What are you reading?" she asked, dropping down into a chair near the window seat.

Kylie made a face and shut the book. "Nothing. I can't concentrate."

Jo nodded understandingly. "I know you're not feeling any better about what happened, but you're *looking* better, healthier."

Kylie smiled wearily. "The future doesn't appear very bright for me, but I've got to be strong—something I've never been."

"Don't be so hard on yourself. You've never had to be strong before, at least not in this way. Actually there aren't many people who have to face what you're having to face." She eyed her sister worriedly. "Honey, I've got another question for you."

"About that night?"

"Yes, in an indirect way. Did Glen ever tell you where he got his drugs?"

"That's a strange question. Why do you want to know?"

"I'll explain in a minute. Did he?"

Kylie shook her head. "That night was the first night I'd ever been around him when I knew for sure he had done drugs."

"What about any of your other friends? Do you know if any of them ever did drugs and where they might have gotten them?"

"A lot of people I know have tried drugs."

She couldn't hide the dismay she felt at that statement.

"I'm sorry, Jo. It's just the way it is. All you have to do is turn around and there are drugs if you want them. The night of the Seaberg party was the first time *I* ever tried any, but most of my friends are way ahead of me in that regard."

Jo bit her lip to keep herself from blurting out her thoughts on the matter of drugs. Later, she promised herself, and then she'd see what she could do to help the rest of the kids in the area. But for now, she had to keep focused on Brett. "Do you know where they get the drugs?"

"No, not really. Why, Jo? What's this all about?"

She was going to have to trust that Kylie was ready to hear the truth. "Honey, I hired a private investigator to find out what he could for me about Brett."

"Why? Does it have something to do with a prenuptial?"

She shook her head. "Brett has refused to sign one."

"Whoa. Sin is not going to go for that."

"Ultimately Sin will go for whatever I decide. But that's not why I hired the investigator." She drew in a deep breath. "Kylie, Brett is not to be trusted. In fact, it appears he's been supplying drugs to your friends."

Kylie's eyes widened incredulously. "Are you sure? You *know* what he did for me."

"I know what he *said* he did for you."

"But you're going to marry . . ." Kylie's expression cleared. "Oh, Lord, I've been incredibly stupid, haven't I? You don't really love Brett. You never did."

"You're not stupid, Kylie. Naive, maybe, but not stupid. Anyone would have been traumatized when faced with the same set of circumstances."

"What happened? Tell me everything."

"I'm not sure of all the facts yet, but Brett did blackmail me into saying I would marry him."

"By promising to tell what I did if you didn't."

"That's right."

Kylie shut her eyes. "I'm so sorry, Jo."

"It's all right, honey. Don't worry about me. I agreed in order to buy time. So that you could get back on your feet. And so that I could make sure of what really happened."

"What do you mean what really happened?"

"I have had a lot of questions about what happened, right from the beginning. And most of my questions are about Brett's involvement."

"Yet you agreed to marry him."

"I had to do that so he'd be quiet and give us some breathing space."

"But you had to play the engagement completely straight."

"Yes." It hadn't been that hard until Cale had come on the scene, she remembered. "Brett's insistence we marry almost immediately didn't bother me too much, because we never had a lot of time anyway. In fact we've taken more time than we should. Glen's parents have to be told the truth."

Kylie straightened. "You're right. It's time I grew up whether I'm ready to or not. I'm going to turn myself in."

Jo looked at her sister with pride and love. "You've come a long way, sweetheart, but I'm

not ready for you to pay for something you
may not have done."

"What are you talking about? I killed
Glen."

"Even if you did, you were acting in self-
defense. In fact, the right thing would have
been for us to have gone to the police immediately and tell them everything." Except Kylie
had been coming apart that night and for days
afterward. And Jo hadn't been sure they'd be
able to prove self-defense. Lord, looking back,
she had handled it all wrong. But when Brett
had told her he had taken care of everything,
she had given in for Kylie's sake and taken the
breathing space he offered. But she'd never
meant it to be more than just breathing space.

"Sometimes I think I should have just let
him—" Kylie began.

"Don't even think it. You can't go back.
You acted instinctively."

"As instinctively as I could on drugs. I have
no excuse, Jo. I'll never forgive myself. Never."

"Hush, Kylie." She reached for her hand
and held it tight. "Something is not adding up
with your story and Brett's."

"But I told you. Some of it is fuzzy to me."

"I know, but just give me a little more time
before you do anything like talking to the police."

Kylie subsided back against the big pillow

and regarded her quietly. "Where does Cale Whitfield come into all this?"

"Ah, Cale." She grimaced. "Well, it's like this. I'm afraid I've fallen in love with him."

"Love? Afraid?"

"Wrong time, wrong place, etc."

"No kidding, wrong time." Kylie thought for a moment. "He *seems* . . . nice. He was trying to connect with me, but . . ." Her words trailed off.

"I'm going to tell him everything, Kylie."

"You can't, Jo!"

"I have to, honey. For my own sanity, for my own sake. I've run out of ways to maneuver around his questions, plus I just can't lie to him anymore. I don't *want* to do it anymore." She paused, then grinned slightly. "Once I tell him, he may turn and run the other way as fast as he can, and I won't have to worry about him anymore. But, Kylie, he won't do anything to hurt you. I promise you."

"How can you know that?"

"I just do. I'm going to find him now. Maybe he can even offer a fresh viewpoint. Lord knows I've run out of ways to look at it." She paused and studied her sister. "Okay?"

Kylie exhaled heavily, then nodded. "Okay. It's time you thought about yourself. Do whatever is best for you."

As it turned out she couldn't speak with Cale as soon as she wanted to. The moment she stepped out of Kylie's room the world caught up with her. Margaret, in a navy hat adorned with a polka-dot bow, insisted she needed to discuss some vital last-minute details for the wedding. Abigail had some family news. Her own assistant called to say there was a stack of faxes waiting in her studio that had to be dealt with immediately. Even Brett called to chat, no doubt to feel out her mood. But no matter, she had to remain as amicable as possible. The last thing she wanted was for him to be on his guard.

From time to time she caught a glimpse of Cale in the distance, but he always seemed to be busy as well. And in the end she didn't get an opportunity to seek him out until well after dinner.

As soon as she walked into the guest house Cale took her in his arms and kissed her. Being wrapped in his arms, in his scent, in his body heat, was just what she'd needed, though she hadn't realized it until that moment. She let herself relax against him and go completely pliant. It was the first time all day she had let down her guard, the first time she had allowed herself not to worry, even for a short time.

"I thought you'd never get here," he muttered when he finally released her.

She looked up at him, certain her heart was in her eyes. "To tell you the truth, after this morning I wasn't sure you'd want to see me."

"Now why in the world would you think that?"

He took her hand and drew her onto the couch with him. Even though the night was mild, he had built a small fire. Its heat felt good on her bare legs. She wished they could spend the night making love, but there were things she had to tell him, difficult things, hard-to-understand things. And after she finished all bets were off. She had no idea what he would do or say.

"I owe you an apology."

"What for?"

"For Brett."

His gaze slowly sharpened. "What's up, Jo?"

She looked down at her hands resting on her lap, fingers entwined.

"Jo?" With a thumb beneath her chin, he lifted her face. "What's wrong?"

"Just about everything."

"Me and you?" He dropped his hand, and his face hardened. "Are you about to tell me this is the last time you'll be seeing me alone?"

"No."

He relaxed. "Then it can't be that bad."

"It's bad enough that you may tell me this is the last time you'll see me alone."

He eyed her thoughtfully. "You're wrong on that count, but let's hear it anyway."

And so she told him. Slowly. Laboriously. Every detail she could think of. She couldn't begin to guess what he was thinking. He didn't interrupt her once, though there were times she wished he would. Anything would be better than his intense silence. Finally she finished. Several excruciating moments passed.

"Why didn't you tell me this before?" he asked at last.

"I didn't see any reason to. It was my problem. It still is, actually."

"Jo"—he exhaled heavily—"I don't know whether to shake you or strangle you."

"Interesting options, but you don't have to do either. In fact there's *nothing* you have to do."

"Did it ever occur to you that I could help?"

"No."

"You didn't feel the matter fell within my expertise?" The anger and frustration beneath the softness of his voice was like thunder.

"First of all, Kylie made me promise not to tell anyone, not even the family. If she didn't want them to know, she certainly wouldn't have wanted a stranger to know. And secondly, as I said, it was *my* problem. My sister—her future—is at stake, and I had to decide the best way to handle it. In retrospect, I did a really lousy job."

"You want to hear something?"

She rubbed her head. "I'm not sure."

"If the same thing had happened to one of my sisters, I would have stalled for time just as you did. I'm not even certain I would have asked for help."

"You understand." The thought gave her comfort.

"Yes. But having said that, I wish you'd have told me sooner. And, by the way, why did you tell me now?"

She wrapped her arms around her waist, hugging herself. "After this morning . . ." She'd told him the facts behind Brett and their engagement. But when it came to how she felt about him, she was on far shakier ground.

"After this morning what? You could have gone on stonewalling my questions indefinitely. I probably never would have figured it out."

"You would have known something was wrong when I called off the wedding."

For the first time since she'd started talking, his eyes darkened. "You're not marrying him. You don't love him."

"No."

He slowly let out his breath. "All right, then. What are we going to do?"

"*We?*"

"We. You and I."

Until that moment she hadn't realized how heavy the burden she'd chosen to carry all alone had been. And even though the problem remained, her load felt lighter.

Cale circled the couch and dropped back down beside her. But he didn't say anything right away. As the story she had told him had unfolded, his gut had caught fire with the acid of pure fury. The idea that Saunders had been blackmailing her into an unwanted marriage had put him into a murderous rage. He'd never killed anyone, but at that moment he could understand the compulsion.

Fortunately pure delight balanced the urge. His instincts hadn't been wrong after all. She *was* in trouble, but most importantly she *didn't* love Saunders. With so many conflicting emotions clashing in him it took some time for his system to regain its balance.

"Thank you for telling me," he finally said.

"It got to the point where it was harder to keep it to myself than it was to tell you."

He captured a shining strand of arctic-blond hair between his fingers. "Why was that?"

Her lips twisted wryly. "To say you were persistent on the subject would be an understatement."

"And that's the only reason?"

Nervousness ran through her laugh. "I don't think I've ever run across anyone who asks more questions than you do."

"If you know of another way to get answers, let me know."

Of course there *was* another reason. She just wasn't certain she was ready to tell him what that reason was. Or if she ever would be.

When she said nothing more, he decided to let the matter drop for the time being. "Okay, so let's talk it out. We have Saunders's story that he buried Glen Keenan's body and that he's got the murder weapon, a fireplace poker, stashed somewhere in case he needs it. The threat being that the poker would implicate Kylie and that if you don't marry him he'd use it against her. However, Kylie says she's sure she used a pool cue. And your private investigator has linked Saunders to supplying drugs to the kids around here, including Glen." He paused. "Which most likely means that he supplied Glen with the drugs he was on at the party. He might have even seen him earlier that night."

"So?"

"I don't know. We need to talk to Kylie." He glanced at his watch.

"She went upstairs before I left to come over here."

"This is pretty important."

"I know it is, believe me, but there

wouldn't be anything we could do tonight anyway."

"Okay, then, I suppose we can wait until
morning." He looked at her. "I won't be rough
on her, I promise."

"I know you won't. I wouldn't have told
you if I didn't trust you."

A smile slowly spread across his face. "Better late than never." He stood up and held out
his hand to her. "Let's go to bed. Now that I
know I'm not going to lose you, I want to hold
you."

She took his hand and came to her feet.
"Not going to lose me?"

He threaded his fingers through her hair
until his hands were cupping her head. "I'm
not going to lose you to Saunders. You're not
going to be married to him."

It wasn't the declaration of love she had
been wishing for, but she was tired, too tired to
deal with it right now. "No, I'm not."

"Just know this, Jo—that I wanted you yesterday, I want you today, and I'll want you tomorrow."

She felt her knees go weak. What more
could she ask for? What more could any
woman ask for? Perhaps commitment was
overrated. She'd admitted to herself that she
loved him. She'd trusted him with the knowledge of what Kylie had done. She'd surrendered her body to him. True, he was talking

about sex and what she was feeling was love. But she couldn't deny herself the comfort and the pleasure of being with him tonight.

She had no more arguments, at least for this night. With her hand in his she followed him into the bedroom. There, he undressed them both, then made slow, deliciously sweet love to her.

Afterward, she lay her head on his chest, contented, relaxed. "There's something I want to ask you."

"What's that?"

"Where do you live?" She heard the soft rumble of his chuckle beneath her ear.

"I've bought the old Murphy place out on Evergreen Lane."

"I always liked that place," she said sleepily. "It has a very special character to it."

"I think so, too, and I'm glad you like it."

"So you're going to be living fairly close."

"Yes."

"Life's funny, you know. I've been wondering what would have happened if I'd met you in the Caldwell garden that night under normal circumstances. Do you think you would have asked me out?"

He smoothed his hand over her hair. "I think that I definitely would have."

The steady sound of his heartbeat soothed her. "Where would we have gone?"

"I don't know. Maybe I would have taken

you to my house and cooked dinner for you and served it in front of the fire."

"Sounds wonderful." Her fingers played with the soft hair on his chest. "Then the next night I could have cooked dinner for you." She shifted so that she could trace the features of his face with her fingertips. "And we could have continued seeing each other, learning about each other." She paused. "And you might have even fallen in love with me."

"Yeah," he said softly. "It could have happened that way. But it didn't. And I fell in love with you anyway."

Her heart skipped a beat. She lifted her head and stared down at him. "You did?"

He pushed a strand of her hair behind her ear. "You didn't know. Lord, I thought I'd been pretty damn obvious."

"But you didn't tell me."

"Didn't I?"

She laughed incredulously. "No, you didn't."

He stared at her for a moment. "Now that I know you're not going to marry Saunders, I can actually breathe without feeling like there's a fist imbedded in my gut. And I can even think somewhat straight, something I really haven't done a lot of lately. But I love you, Jo. I love you more than I can say."

Maybe because he was saying exactly what she wanted him to say she couldn't let herself believe what she was hearing. "When did your wanting me turn into love?"

"Probably during our first kiss in the garden. But the wanting was so strong, it pushed everything out of my mind for a while."

"Cale?"

"Hmmmm?"

"I love you too." She laughed joyously and softly at his look of surprise. "You and I have such bad timing. We should have told each other days ago."

He pulled her head down until their lips were touching, and right before he kissed her, he murmured, "I think our timing is exquisite."

The morning sun streamed into Kylie's bedroom as she looked from Jo to Cale then back to Jo. "So you told him."

"Yes, honey, I did. And he's going to help us."

"Help us what? There's nothing anyone can do. Except me, that is." She wrapped her arms around herself. "I've made up my mind. I've got to turn myself in. It's the right thing to do, and it's about time I did something right."

Cale stepped forward. "I'm hoping it won't come to that, Kylie. True, you will have to talk to the police, probably even testify, but let's not think about you turning yourself in."

Her pale hair swished back and forth over her shoulders as she shook her head. "I don't see how it can be avoided. I killed someone. I fell apart after it happened, but now I've finally started to face up to things. I'm not going to let Jo pay for something I did."

"I think that's wonderful, Kylie," he said gently. "And I agree that Jo should be spared. And I can promise you that I'm going to do my best to try to figure out exactly what happened. And to do that I need you to answer a couple of questions."

She looked doubtful. "I've told Jo everything that happened."

"I know you did, but there are one or two things that I'd like to go over again. Tell me what happened from the point where Glen backed you up against the pool table."

"I-I panicked. He had me bent over the pool table . . . his body was pressing down on me . . . he was hurting me." A sob escaped her. Her hand flew to her mouth as if she could pull the sound back.

Jo walked over to Kylie and slipped her arm around her. "Take your time," she said softly.

"What happened then?" Cale prompted.

"I remember grasping behind me for something to help me and finding the pool cue. I swung it at him, and I felt it connect. He made a sound, reached for his head, then staggered backward." She gestured vaguely. "Then he fell, and God, there was so much blood."

"There always is with any head wound, Kylie. Then what happened?"

"I-I think I started to scream. I'm not sure. But Brett came in then."

"Do you know what he was doing around the pool house?"

"No. He told me to leave, go home, that he'd take care of everything. And he did."

"Okay, Kylie, I have only one more question for you. Do you know if there's any type of construction going on at the Seabergs'?"

TEN

Later that night Jo opened the doors of the sitting room to find Brett studying a crystal sculpture in an assessing way, almost, she thought grimly, as if he were thinking of selling it, or pawning it. "Good evening, Brett."

"Ah, there you are, darling." He glanced at his watch. "You know, you're really going to have to make more of an effort to be on time from now on. I don't like to wait on you, and I see no reason why I should."

With a smile she ducked his effort at giving her his usual kiss of greeting. "You're right. You shouldn't."

Her agreement on the issue of punctuality appeared to mollify him and make up for the lack of the kiss.

"Good. I'm glad you agree."

"Oh, I do. And I hope you'll agree with me

that as of this moment we are no longer engaged."

His features contorted with annoyance. "What are you talking about?"

Unwilling to get too close to him, she stripped the diamond from her finger and tossed it to him. "I'm talking about the fact that your blackmail is not going to work anymore. You see, I've figured out what really happened at the Seaberg party."

In the next room, listening as the recorder on a nearby table taped, Cale tensed, ready to rush in if Saunders laid so much as a finger on Jo. Next to him, Lieutenant Robinson put a hand on his shoulder, silently telling him to keep calm. He nodded. He knew as well or better than Lieutenant Robinson how to comport himself under these circumstances. But he'd never been in this situation before, when the woman he loved was in jeopardy.

Brett's brows drew together in a scowl. "I *told* you exactly what happened. There's nothing to figure out."

"Yes, you did tell me, and I listened." She clasped her hands together. It wouldn't do for Brett to see them shake. "So now do me the courtesy of listening to what I think happened."

His scowl increased. "What's brought this on, Joanna? The wedding is just days away."

She shook her head. "No, the wedding is off."

"What in the hell are you talking about?"

He started toward her, and she backed away until he stopped. "It's very simple. You see, I've been trying to piece things together, and I think I've finally gotten it. First of all, it was no surprise to me that you were at the Seaberg party. You've always made it your business to be seen in what you think is the right place at the right time. But on that particular night I never could figure out how you just happened to be near the pool house at that exact moment."

"What difference does it make? Kylie was lucky I was there."

"Actually she was extremely unlucky."

"Joanna—"

"No, just listen." He folded his arms across his chest in an arrogant manner that told her he wasn't taking her seriously, but she forged ahead. "You stepped out of the house to take a break as Kylie had done a few minutes earlier, and you noticed Kylie and Glen heading toward the pool house. Or, more than likely, you were waiting for Glen, since you two had seen each other earlier when you sold him drugs."

He gave a short bark of a laugh. "Now I know you're out of your mind. Drugs, Joanna?"

"Drugs, Brett. I've had you followed for the last two weeks, and I know you're selling drugs." She smiled at the shock on his face. "Did you really think I would let you blackmail me into marriage? I always planned to find a way out."

"There is no way out. Not if you want to protect Kylie."

"There's always a way out. What happened that night, Brett? Did you have a fight with Glen? Did he say he was going to try to clean up his act and turn you in? That would have been very bad for you, wouldn't it? At any rate, you did argue with him over something, and eventually you must have convinced him to take one last ride on drugs. But you weren't through with him, were you? You followed him when he headed for the pool house with Kylie."

"You've got nothing on me. *Nothing.* Everything you just said is pure conjecture."

Cale stared at the recorder. Saunders was right, but it was also true they had a better than average chance of proving that Kylie didn't kill

Glen once they had recovered Glen's body. It *would* be helpful, however, if Saunders would give himself away somehow. He just wished there had been some way he could have confronted Saunders for Jo. And he wished to hell it was all over with. He was worried sick. Saunders was within striking distance of Jo and could hurt her before he could get to her.

"But there's more," Jo said. "So there you were, standing outside the pool house, more than likely watching Kylie and Glen through a window. Glen, who, let me emphasize, was high on drugs he had gotten from *you.*"

"You don't know any of that for sure. You're *guessing.*"

She forced a smile to her face and prayed she looked confident. "Pretty good guess, though, right? And as I said there's more. You saw Glen back Kylie onto that pool table, you saw her hit him with the pool cue and him fall. Talk about luck. Then you rushed in like a knight in shining armor and told her to go home, that you'd take care of everything."

"At least you got that part right. I *helped* your sister."

"Kylie thought Glen was dead, except he wasn't, was he? He wasn't dead until you picked up the fireplace poker and finished the job."

His eyes were narrow slits, and his skin had taken on a pallor. "You've been a busy girl, trying to figure this all out. Unfortunately for you there's no way you can prove that."

"But you're not sure about that, are you? You know, the problem of what you did with Glen's body stumped me for a while. I know where the pool house is located. I also know where you would have parked for the party. There's quite a distance between the two locations. There's no way you could have gotten Glen's body from the pool house to your car without someone seeing you."

"You don't need to know how I did it. All you need to know is that I got the job done and Kylie is safe because of me."

"I asked Kylie if there was any construction going on at the Seaberg estate. And guess what? They were putting in new tennis courts during that time."

The laugh he gave was obviously forced. "So?"

Damn the man, Cale thought. Why didn't he just confess and save them all a lot of trouble? He glanced at Kylie, who was sitting pale and quiet, staring at the recorder. For two weeks she had lived with the thought that she had killed someone. It must have been hell for her. She would come out of this all right, he thought, but she would be a different person. From what she had said to him, it seemed she had already started to grow up.

"It's all over, Brett," Jo said. "According to Kylie, the Seabergs were spreading the word that night about the new courts. They were planning another party when they were finished, and you would have heard that. In fact I can probably prove that by asking around."

"I don't care what you can and can't prove. You and I are going to marry, just as I planned. And I'm going to get a seat on the board, just as I planned."

"Really? And what are you going to do when I ask the Seabergs if I can tear up their new tennis courts to see if that's where you buried Glen?"

For the first time color drained from his face. "You're bluffing. The Seabergs would never let you do that."

"They would if I offered to pay for the entire thing, plus the cost of new courts. They would if it would mean finding Glen."

"No, no, you're wrong."

"When I thought about it, I remembered that there was a low place where they were putting the tennis courts. I bet you remembered it too."

"So what?"

"So they would have had to grade the land. You carried Glen there and put him in that low place, an effective shallow grave. Then you shoved just enough dirt and branches over him to cover him. Another stroke of luck, right? There was going to be several tons of dirt pushed over that place within the next few days, and you knew it."

"Pure speculation. It doesn't matter anyway. The tennis courts have been poured. I checked. And they won't let you tear it up."

She resisted the urge to smile. "And why did you check the tennis courts, Brett? Because you wanted to make sure that no one would find Glen?"

"And no one will, either. Because nothing has changed. Your sister can still be implicated." He started toward her again.

"Ah, but you forgot something."

Her words stopped him. "What?"

"The fireplace poker. You buried it with Glen, didn't you?"

"No, I told you—"

"Carrying it would have given you the same problem as Glen's body. Someone would have seen you, so the simplest thing would have been to bury it with Glen. And you made another mistake. Kylie hit Glen with the pool cue. I'm sure it stunned him for a moment, enough to make him go down, but it didn't kill him. She wouldn't be strong enough to swing a blow hard enough to kill him, not with a pool cue. She also wouldn't be strong enough to carry him to the site of the new courts."

"You're wrong. She killed him with the fireplace poker."

She shook her head. "*You* did. As for the pool cue, even if you thought to wipe the blood off, there'll still be traces, plus her fingerprints. And her fingerprints aren't on the poker, are they? Yours are."

"You think I'd be stupid enough to leave my fingerprints on it?"

"You might have been. I'm sure you were in a hurry. Or you might have wiped some off and left others on. Luckily for us, there'll also be forensic evidence on Glen."

"You think you've got it all figured out, don't you? You think you're off the hook?"

"I know I am. There's only one thing I don't know. Why? Did you kill Glen because you saw the opportunity to get into our family? Or was it something more? Like the fact that you were supplying drugs to Glen and he had threatened to turn you in? Or a combination of both? Two birds with one stone."

"I don't know what you're talking about."

"It doesn't matter. I'm going to see that the tennis court is dug up. Poor Glen will be there, along with the weapon. Forensics will be able to prove which weapon killed him, which in turn will prove you did it."

"Damn you!" Hatred burned in his eyes. "You and your whole damn family think you're too good for ordinary people like me. But you can be trapped like anyone else. And I can still pin Glen's murder on Kylie."

"Really? How?"

"When she was struggling with Glen in the pool house, a barrette came out of her hair. I buried it with Glen. Even if they do let you dig up his body, the police will find it and they'll think it fell there when she buried him."

She smiled. "That's very interesting. Why don't you explain all of that to Lieutenant Robinson?"

"That's right," the lieutenant said, coming into the room. "I'd like to hear it."

Cale was a half step behind him. He went straight to her and took her in his arms.

Brilliant crimsons, oranges, and golds flamed across the sky later that day as the sun sank slowly over the horizon. Cale found Jo standing on the back terrace, gazing at the spectacle. He came up behind her and put his hands on her shoulders. "How are you doing?"

She leaned back against him. It felt so good to let herself lean on him and be supported by him. "Fine. I'm just glad it's all over."

"Where's Kylie?"

"She's upstairs. Abigail is talking with her."

She gave a light laugh. "Abigail is quite upset with herself that she didn't know what was going on."

"She suspected something was wrong, but no one would have been able to imagine or guess the scenario that was happening."

"That's certainly the truth."

He bent his head and pressed his mouth against her ear. "So what now?"

"What do you mean?"

"It looks like I'm out of a job. The wedding is canceled."

Her hand flew to her forehead. "Oh, my Lord. I've got to cancel everything."

He turned her around to him. "It should be easy. Just tell the hat lady."

"Margaret? Yes, she can handle the orchestra, the florist, and the other suppliers. But the guests, my cousins—they'll all have to be notified."

"Sounds like a lot of trouble."

"What will be hard will be the explanation. I'll tell my cousins the truth, of course, but the guests—"

"I have an idea. Why not have the wedding go on as planned?"

She looked at him blankly. "What?"

He shrugged. "It would be a shame to disappoint everyone."

"My cousins won't be disappointed when they realize that if the wedding had gone off as planned, I would be married to a murderer and a blackmailer."

"I agree they wouldn't want you to marry someone wrong. But how about someone who is very much in love with you and couldn't care less who your family is?"

Her heart skipped a beat. "Cale?"

He smiled. "Smart girl."

"You want to marry me?"

"So much so, I don't think I'll take no for an answer."

With a joyous laugh she threw her arms around him. "I know what we can do. We can hand out cards to the guests as they arrive that say, *The part of the groom will be played today by Cale Whitfield.*"

"Make it say, *today, tomorrow, and for the rest of our lives,* and you've got a deal."

Happiness filled her eyes with tears. "That sounds perfect."

"There's just one thing."

"After all we've been through you mean there's only *one* thing?"

"I can't give you a ten-carat diamond or however big that ring was that Saunders gave you."

"Cale, that's so unimportant—"

"But I have an idea."

She grinned. "Well, I loved your first idea."

"I'll give you a one-carat diamond on our wedding day, and I'll give you a one-carat diamond every year on our anniversary, and in fifty years, on our golden anniversary, you'll have fifty diamonds."

She laughed. "My fingers aren't going to be able to hold all those diamonds."

"That's okay. I'll find other places on your body to put them."

She laughed again, so happy, she couldn't stop. "But they'll weigh me down. I won't be able to move."

He grinned. "That's okay, because you'll be in bed, right where I want you."

"Even after fifty years?"

"Even after sixty years. Even after seventy years. I'll always want you, Jo. Always."

With a sigh of pure bliss, she went back into his arms. "I can't wait for you to meet my family."

He laughed. "And I can't wait for you to meet my sisters. You're not going to know what hit you."

"I already feel that way," she murmured. "And I love the feeling."

THE EDITORS'
CORNER

When renowned psychic Fiona hosts a special radio call-in show promising to reveal the perfect woman for the man who won't commit, four listeners' lives are forever changed. So begins our AMERICAN BACHELORS romances next month! You'll be captivated by these red, white, and blue hunks who are exactly the kind of men your mother warned you about. Each one knows just the right moves to seduce, dazzle, and entice, and it will take the most bewitching of heroines to conquer our sexy heroes' resistant hearts. But with the help of destiny and passion, these die-hard AMERICAN BACHELORS won't be single much longer.

Riley Morse creates a sizzling tale of everlasting love in **KISS OF FIRE**, LOVESWEPT #766. He'd been warned—and tempted—by the mysterious promise that his fate was linked to a lady whose caress would strike sparks, but Dr. Dayton Westfield knows that playing with fire is his only hope! When Adrienne Bellew enters his lab, he feels the heat of her need in his blood—and answers it with insatiable hunger. Weaving the tantalizing mysteries of a woman's sensual power with the fierce passion of a man who'd give anything to believe in the impossible, Riley Morse presents this fabulous follow-up to her sensational Loveswept debut.

Victoria Leigh turns up the heat in this breathlessly sexy, faster-than-a-bullet story of love on the run, **NIGHT OF THE HAWK,** LOVESWEPT #767. She'd pointed a gun at his head, yet never fired the weapon—but Hawk believes the woman must have been hired to kill him! Angela Ferguson bravely insists she knows nothing, no matter how dark his threats, but even her innocence won't save her from the violence that shadows his haunted eyes. When a renegade with vengeance on his mind meets a feisty heroine who's more than his match, be prepared for anything—Victoria Leigh always packs a passionate punch.

THRILL OF THE CHASE, LOVESWEPT #768, showcases the playful, witty, and very sexy writing of Maris Soule. He's a heartbreaker, a hunk whose sex appeal is hard to ignore, but Peggi Barnett is tired of men who thrill to the chase, then never seem willing to catch what they've pursued! Cameron Slater is gorgeous, charming, and enjoys teasing the woman he's hired to redo his home. He'd always vowed that marriage wasn't on his agenda, but could she be the woman he'd been waiting for all his life? When a pretty designer finds that a handshake feels more like an embrace, Maris Soule sets a delicious game in motion.

Praised by *Romantic Times* as "a magnificent writer," Terry Lawrence presents **DRIVEN TO DISTRACTION**, LOVESWEPT #769. Cole Creek is almost too much man to spend a month with in the confines of a car, Evie Mercer admits, but sitting too close for comfort next to him will certainly make the miles fly! Sharing tight quarters with a woman he's fallen head-over-heels for isn't such a good idea, especially when a tender kiss explodes into pure, primal yearning. Terry Lawrence knows just how to entangle smart, sexy women with an appetite for all life offers with the kind of men the best dreams are made of.

Happy reading!

With warmest wishes,

Beth de Guzman

Shauna Summers

Beth de Guzman

Shauna Summers

Senior Editor

Associate Editor

P.S. Watch for these fascinating Bantam women's fiction titles coming in December: With her spell-binding imagination and seductive voice, Kay Hooper is the only author worthy of being called today's successor to Victoria Holt; now, she has created a unique and stunning tale of contemporary suspense that begins with a mysterious homecoming and ends in a shattering explosion of passion, greed, and murder—and all because a stranger says her name is **AMANDA.** *New York Times* bestselling author Sandra Brown's **HEAVEN'S PRICE** will be available in paperback, and Katherine O'Neal, winner of the *Romantic Times* Award for Best Sensual Historical Romance, unveils **MASTER OF PARADISE**—a tantalizing tale of a notorious pirate, a rebellious beauty, and a dangerously erotic duel of hearts. Finally, in the bestselling tradition of Arnette Lamb and Pamela Morsi, **TEXAS OUTLAW** is a triumph of captivating romance and adventure from spectacular newcomer Adrienne deWolfe. Be sure to catch next month's LOVESWEPTs for a preview of these wonderful novels. And immediately following this page, catch a glimpse of the outstanding Bantam women's fiction titles on sale *now*!

Don't miss these extraordinary books
by your favorite Bantam authors

On sale in October:

BRAZEN
by Susan Johnson

THE REDHEAD
AND
THE PREACHER
by Sandra Chastain

THE QUEST
by Juliana Garnett

"Susan Johnson is one of the best!"
—*Romantic Times*

BRAZEN

by bestselling author
Susan Johnson

*Countess Angela de Grae seemed to have everything a
woman could want: wealth, position, and an exquisite
beauty that had once bewitched even the Prince of Wales.
But from the moment the dashing American playboy and
adventurer Kit Braddock laid eyes on the legendary Countess Angel, he knew she was unlike the other rich, jaded blue
bloods he'd ever met. For beneath the polish and glitter of
her privileged life, he glimpsed a courageous woman tor-
mented by a secret heartache. Determined to uncover the
real Angela de Grae, what Kit found was a passionate soul
mate trapped in a dangerous situation by a desperate man.
And in one moment of reckless, stolen pleasure, Kit would
pledge his very life to rescue her and give her the one thing
she'd forbidden herself: the ecstasy of true love.*

"How can we leave? Bertie's still here," Angela replied with a small sigh. No one could precede a royal
guest.

Kit's eyes shone with mischief. "I *could* lower you
over the balustrade and we could *both* escape."

Her mouth quirked faintly in a tentative smile.
"How tempting. Are the festivities wearing thin for
you too, Mr. Braddock? We were supposed to for-

mally meet tonight," she graciously added. "I'm Angela de Grae, a good friend of Priscilla's mother."

"I thought so," he neutrally replied. He silently commended her for the subtle insinuation of the name of the young woman he'd been seeing lately, and thought her gracious for not flaunting her celebrity. She was a professional beauty; her photos sold in enormous numbers in England. "And yes, worn thin is a very polite expression for my current mood. I'm racing early tomorrow and I'd rather sleep tonight than watch everyone become increasingly drunk."

"Champagne *is* flowing in torrents, but Bertie is pleased with his victory. Especially after losing to his nephew last year."

"Willie deserved his trouncing today. He should have been disqualified for almost shearing off our bow on the turn. But at the moment I'm only concerned with escaping from the party. If I'm going to have my crew in shape in the morning, we're all going to need some rest."

"Do they wait for your return?" The countess's voice held the smallest hint of huskiness, an unconsciously flirtatious voice.

"Priscilla doesn't know, of course." Kit Braddock referred to his female companions as crew; reportedly he kept a small harem on board his yacht to entertain him on his journeys around the world.

"She's too young to know," he casually replied, "and rumor probably exaggerates."

The countess took note of the equivocal adverb but she too understood the demands of politesse and said, "Yes, I'm sure," to both portions of his statement. It was very much a man's world in which she lived, and while her enormous personal wealth had always allowed her a greater measure of freedom than that allowed other women, even Angela de Grae had at times to recognize the stark reality of the double standard.

"Well then?" His deep voice held a teasing query.

"I'm not sure my mopish brooding is worth a broken leg," Angela pleasantly retorted, rising from her chair and moving the small distance to the balustrade. Gazing over the climbing roses, she swiftly contemplated the drop to the ground. "Are you very strong? I certainly hope so," she quickly added, hoisting herself up on the balustrade and smoothly swinging her legs and lacy skirts over the side. "Although, Mr. Braddock," she went on in a delectable drawl, smiling at him from over her bare shoulder, "you certainly *look* like you have the strength to rescue us from this tedious evening."

How old *was* she? he found himself suddenly wondering. She looked like a young girl perched on the terrace rail, her hands braced to balance herself. In the next quicksilver instant he decided it didn't matter. And in a flashing moment more he was responding to the smile that had charmed a legion of men since young "Angel" Lawton had first smiled up at her grandpapa from the cradle and Viscount Lawton decided to overlook his scapegrace son in his will and leave his fortune to his beautiful granddaughter.

"Wait," Kit said, apropos her pose and other more disturbing sensations engendered by the countess's tempting smile. Leaping down onto the grass bordering the flower beds, he gingerly stepped between the tall stands of lilies, stopped directly below her, lifted his arms, smiled, and said, "Now."

Without hesitation she jumped in a flurry of petticoats and handmade lace and fell into his arms.

THE REDHEAD
AND THE
PREACHER

by award-winning author

Sandra Chastain

"This delightful author has a tremendous talent that places her on a pinnacle reserved for special romance writers."
—*Affaire de Coeur*

McKenzie Kathryn Calhoun didn't mean to rob the bank in Promise, Kansas. But when she accidentally did, she didn't think, she ran. Suddenly the raggedy tomboy the town rejected had the money to make a life for herself . . . if she didn't get caught. But it was just her luck to find herself sitting across the stagecoach from a dangerously handsome, gun-toting preacher who seemed to see through her bravado to the desperate woman beneath.

Assuming the identity of the minister had seemed a ready-made cover for his mission. Now, in the coach, he amused himself by listening, feeling, allowing his mind's eye to discover the identity of his traveling companion.

Female, he confirmed. The driver had called her ma'am.

A good build and firm step, because the carriage

had tilted as she stepped inside, and she'd settled herself without a lot of swishing around.

Probably no-nonsense, for he could see the tips of her boots beneath the brim of his hat. The boots were worn, though the clothing looked new. The only scent in the air was that of the dye in the cloth.

Practical, for she'd planted both feet firmly on the floor of the coach and hadn't moved them; no fidgeting or fussing with herself.

Deciding that she seemed safe enough, he flicked the brim of his hat back and took a look at her.

Wrong, on all four counts. Dead wrong. She was sitting quietly, yes, but that stillness was born of sheer determination—no, more like desperation. She was looking down at rough, red hands and holding on to her portmanteau as if she dared anybody to touch it. Her eyes weren't closed, but they might as well have been.

The stage moved away in a lumbering motion as it picked up speed.

The woman didn't move.

Finally, after an hour of steady galloping by the horses pulling the stagecoach, she let out a deep breath and appeared to relax.

"Looks like you got away," he said.

"What?" She raised a veil of sooty lashes to reveal huge eyes as green as the moss along the banks of the Mississippi River where he'd played as a child. Something about her was all wrong. The set of her lips was meant to challenge. But beneath that bravado he sensed an appealing uncertainty that softened the lines in her forehead.

"Back there you looked as if you were running away from home and were afraid you wouldn't escape," he said.

"I was," she said.

"Pretty risky, a woman alone. No traveling companion, no family?"

"Don't have any, buried my—the last—companion back in Promise."

Macky risked taking a look at the man across from her. He was big, six feet of black, beginning with his boots and ending with the patch over his eye and a hat that cast a shadow over a face etched by a two-day growth of beard. There was an impression of quiet danger in the casual way he seemed to look straight through her as if he knew that she was an impostor and was waiting for her to confess.

Across the carriage, Bran was aware of the girl's scrutiny. He felt himself giving her a reluctant grin. She was a feisty one, his peculiar-looking companion with wisps of hot red hair trying to escape her odd little hat. She had a strong face and a wide mouth. But what held him were green eyes that, no matter how frosty she tried to make them, still shimmered with sparks of silver lightning.

"I'm called Bran," he said slowly.

Bran decided she was definitely running away from something, but he couldn't figure what. He should back off. Planning the job waiting for him in Heaven was what he ought to be doing.

Bran had always found women ready to make a casual relationship with him more personal. They seemed attracted to danger. But this one didn't. And that cool independence had become a challenge.

Maybe a little conversation would shake the uneasy feeling that he was experiencing.

"What are you called?" he asked.

"Trouble mostly," she said with a sigh that told him more than she'd intended.

"That's an odd name for a woman."

"That's as good as you're going to get," she added, lifting a corner of the shade covering the open window.

Good? There it was again. "Good is a rare quality in my life." He took a long look at her. "But I'm willing to reserve judgment."

He was doing it again—extending the conversation. Something about this young woman was intriguing. "Truth is, I'm a lot more likely to appreciate a woman who's bad. Wake me when we get to the way station."

THE QUEST
by dazzling new talent
Juliana Garnett

"An opulent and sensuous tale of unbridled
passions. I couldn't stop reading."
—Bertrice Small, author of *The Love Slave*

*All his life, the notorious Rolf of Dragonwyck, known as
the Dragon, has taken what he wanted by the strength of
his sword and the fierceness of his spirit. But now his
enemies have found the chink in his armor: his beloved
son. With the boy held prisoner by the ruthless Earl of
Seabrook, the Dragon will do anything to get him back.
Yet when he decides to trade a hostage for a hostage and
takes the beautiful Lady Annice d'Arcy captive, the sea-
soned knight is in for a shock: far from the biddable maiden
he expects, he finds himself saddled with a recklessly defi-
ant lady who has a rather dangerous effect on his body
and his soul. Suddenly, the fearless Dragon wonders if he
might win back his child . . . only to lose his warrior's
heart.*

Uneasy at his seeming indifference to her presence,
Annice made no protest or comment when Vachel
brought her a stool and seated her between Sir Guy
and le Draca. The high table was at a right angle to
the other tables lining two sides of the hall, giving an
excellent vantage point. A fire burned in the middle.
Supper was usually a light meal, coming as it did after

evensong and sunset. It was still the Lenten season so platters of meat were replaced by broiled fish and trenchers of fish stew. Cheeses and white bread made up for the lack of meat. There was no lack of spiced wine, with cups readily refilled. Intricate subtleties were brought out for the admiration and inspection of the delighted guests. One subtlety was constructed of towering pastry and glazed honey in the shape of a castle complete with jellied moat.

'Twas obvious that the lord of Dragonwyck was not close or mean with his food, as if he did not suspect a siege might soon be laid at his walls. Any other lord might be frugal at such a time, fearing long abstinence from ready supplies.

Even the beggars common in every hall were being doled out fresh foods along with scraps; Annice saw servants burdened with huge baskets leave the hall. Frowning, she toyed with her spoon instead of eating. Was this show of abundance supposed to impress her with his indifference? Or had he already received an answer to his proposal, and knew he would not have to wage war?

Looking up hopefully, Annice noted le Draca's gaze resting on her. Thick lashes shadowed his eyes, hiding any possible clue, though a faint smile tugged at the corners of his mouth. He was too serene, too confident. He must know something. A courier could well have traveled to Seabrook and come back with a reply in a fortnight.

Her heart gave an erratic thump. P'r'aps she was about to be released. . . . Had negotiations been completed to that end?

She had her answer in the next moment, when he

leaned close to her to say, "I trust you will enjoy your stay with us, milady, for it seems that it will be an extended one."

The breath caught in her throat. One hand rose as of its own accord, fingers going to her mouth to still any impulsive reply. She stared at him. His lashes lifted, and she saw in the banked green fires of his eyes that he was furious. Dismay choked her, and she was barely aware of the intent, curious gazes fixed on them as she half rose from her stool.

Catching her arm, he pulled her back down none too gently. "Nay, do not think to flee. You are well and truly snared, little fox. It seems that your overlord prefers the hostage he has for the one I have. Or so he claims. Will he be so self-satisfied with his decision in the future, I wonder? Though I will not harm you, for concern that he might think it politic to do harm to my son, there are varying degrees of subjugation."

His hand stroked up her arm, brushing the green velvet of her gown in a slow, languorous caress that made her stiffen. One of her long strands of hair had fallen over her shoulder to drape her breast, and the backs of his fingers rubbed against her as he lifted the heavy rope of hair in his palm. He did not move his hand, but allowed it to remain pressed against her breast as he twisted the strands of hair entwined with ribbons between his thumb and fingers. Staring at her with a thoughtful expression, he slowly began to wind the bound hair around his hand to bring her even closer to him.

Annice wanted to resist, but knew that 'twas useless, even in front of the assemblage. None would stay their overlord. Helpless, she found herself almost in his lap, her face mere inches from his and her hands braced against his chest.

"It seems," Rolf murmured softly, his words obviously intended for her ears alone, "that your overlord regards me in the role of abductor rather than captor. Though there may seem to be little difference 'tween the two, there is a significant one. As abductor of a widowed female, I will be required to pay penance as well as a fine for taking you." An unpleasant smile slanted his mouth and curdled her blood. "Unless, of course, I receive permission from your next of kin—in this case, your brother."

"My . . . my brother?" Annice struggled for words. "But I have not corresponded with Aubert in years. We barely know one another, and—permission for what?"

Still holding her hair so that her face was unnervingly close, he grasped her chin in his other hand, fingers cradling her in a loose grip. P'r'aps she should have been better prepared. After all, it was not unheard of, though times had passed when it was common.

Still, Annice was totally taken aback when le Draca said in a rolling growl, "Permission to wed you, milady."

Don't miss these sensational romances
from Bantam Books, on sale in
November:

AMANDA
by Kay Hooper

HEAVEN'S PRICE
by Sandra Brown

MASTER OF PARADISE
by Katherine O'Neal

TEXAS OUTLAW
by Adrienne deWolfe

DON'T MISS THESE FABULOUS BANTAM WOMEN'S FICTION TITLES

On Sale in October

BRAZEN
by bestselling author SUSAN JOHNSON
"No one [but Susan Johnson] can write such
rousing love stories." —*Rendezvous*

Susan Johnson "is one of the best!" declares *Romantic Times*. And in
this sizzling new novel, the award-winning, bestselling author of *Pure
Sin* and *Outlaw* entices us once more into a world of sensual fantasy.

_____ 57213-X $5.99/$7.99

THE REDHEAD AND THE PREACHER
by award-winning author SANDRA CHASTAIN
"This delightful author has a tremendous talent that
places her on a pinnacle reserved for special
romance writers." —*Affaire de Coeur*

A lighthearted, fast-paced western romance from bestselling Sandra
Chastain, who is making this kind of romance her own.

_____ 56863-9 $5.50/$6.99

THE QUEST
by dazzling new talent JULIANA GARNETT
"An opulent and sensuous tale of unbridled passions. I couldn't
stop reading." —Bertrice Small, author of *The Love Slave*

A spellbinding tale of treachery, chivalry, and dangerous temptation in
the medieval tradition of Bertrice Small, Virginia Henley, and Arnette
Lamb.

_____ 56861-2 $5.50/$6.99

Ask for these books at your local bookstore or use this page to order.

Please send me the books I have checked above. I am enclosing $_____ (add $2.50 to
cover postage and handling). Send check or money order, no cash or C.O.D.'s, please.

Name _____

Address _____

City/State/Zip _____

Send order to: Bantam Books, Dept. FN158, 2451 S. Wolf Rd., Des Plaines, IL 60018
Allow four to six weeks for delivery.
Prices and availability subject to change without notice.   FN 158 10/95

DON'T MISS THESE FABULOUS
BANTAM WOMEN'S FICTION TITLES

On Sale in November

AMANDA *by bestselling author* Kay Hooper

*"Don't miss a story that will keep your reading light on until
well into the night."*—Catherine Coulter

With her spellbinding imagination and seductive voice, Kay Hooper is the
only author worthy of being called today's successor to Victoria Holt. Now
this powerful storyteller has created a stunning tale of contemporary suspense that begins with a mysterious homecoming and ends in a shattering
explosion of passion, greed, and murder.____ 09957-4 $19.95/$24.95 in Canada

MASTER OF PARADISE *by* Katherine O'Neal

Winner of *Romantic Times'* Best Sensual Historical Romance
Award for THE LAST HIGHWAYMAN

*"Katherine O'Neal is the queen of romantic adventure,
reigning over a court of intrigue, sensuality, and good
old-fashioned storytelling."*—Affaire de Coeur

Katherine O'Neal unveils a spectacular new novel of romantic adventure—
a tantalizing tale of a notorious pirate, a rebellious beauty, and a dangerously erotic duel of hearts.   ____ 56956-2 $5.50/$7.99

TEXAS OUTLAW *by sparkling new talent* Adrienne deWolfe

Combining the delightful wit of Arnette Lamb and the tender emotion of
Pamela Morsi, this spectacular historical romance is a dazzling debut from
an author destined to be a star.   ____ 57395-0 $4.99/$6.99

New York Times bestselling author Sandra Brown's

HEAVEN'S PRICE

Now available in paperback ____ 57157-5 $5.50/$6.99

- -

Ask for these books at your local bookstore or use this page to order.

Please send me the books I have checked above. I am enclosing $____ (add $2.50 to
cover postage and handling). Send check or money order, no cash or C.O.D.'s, please.

Name _____

Address _____

City/State/Zip _____

Send order to: Bantam Books, Dept. FN159, 2451 S. Wolf Rd., Des Plaines, IL 60018
Allow four to six weeks for delivery.

Prices and availability subject to change without notice.   FN 159 11/95